The Charm Tree

To the staff at the TLC,
Thanks so much for the happy memories. It's been a great pleasure working with you all!

Heather Bax

The Charm Tree

Book One of the Shansymoon Series

Heather Ray Bax

Order this book online at www.trafford.com
or email orders@trafford.com

Most Trafford titles are also available at major online book retailers.

© Copyright 2010 Heather Ray Bax.
All rights reserved. No part of this publication may be reproduced, stored
in a retrieval system, or transmitted, in any form or by any means, electronic,
mechanical, photocopying, recording, or otherwise, without
the written prior permission of the author.

Photographs by Dale Northey

Printed in Victoria, BC, Canada.

ISBN: 978-1-4269-2860-4 (sc)

*Our mission is to efficiently provide the world's finest, most comprehensive
book publishing service, enabling every author to experience success.
To find out how to publish your book, your way, and have it available
worldwide, visit us online at www.trafford.com*

Trafford rev. 4/21/2010

Trafford PUBLISHING® www.trafford.com

North America & international
toll-free: 1 888 232 4444 (USA & Canada)
phone: 250 383 6864 ♦ fax: 812 355 4082

For Tracy, Melody, Rowen and Gaelan:
The stars are not so very far away;
never stop reaching!

Acknowledgements

My deepest thanks to Dallas Hortness, Shirley Hortness, Kathy Bax and Don Macdonald for your continued love and support. My gratitude to Cathy Cobey, Richard Fancy, Kathleen O'Connor, Jason Forde, Lynne McKechnie, Catherina Shapko, Jill Baryluk and Chris Groeneboer for reading my manuscript and giving me your valuable feedback. Many thanks to Dale Northey for your photography magic. My eternal gratitude to my husband Ryan Bax for always believing in me. Special thanks to the Fairies, who kept poking and prodding me until this book was finished. Ouch! It's done—leave me alone!

★ 1 ★
Megan's Nightmare

It was Thursday, and it was as a Thursday ought to be—cold, wet and dreary. As Megan walked home from school on that miserable November afternoon through the icy drizzle, she scrunched her neck down as far as it would go into her jacket and dug her hands deep into her pockets. She felt like kicking herself for forgetting her umbrella again.

It had been Megan's last day at Shadyville Public School, and she had never thought that she would regret leaving that horrid place. Megan wouldn't miss Kendra Karson or her crowd of snobbish, prissy followers. She wouldn't miss taking a quick turn into the girls' washroom or hiding behind locker doors until the girls had passed. But now Megan could think of far worse things— moving across the country and starting a new school in the middle of the year for one. What would be waiting for her in the new place? Megan didn't want to think about it. It gave her a queer feeling, like there was a deep, black puddle in the pit of her stomach.

As Megan rounded the last block, she caught sight of the house she had grown up in. It had pale yellow siding and a large, white porch. Megan's mother Laura Whittlebee had a passion for gardening, and she had landscaped the front yard with towering trees, winding paths and twisting vines.

The yard also boasted a large scarecrow in a silver spaceman suit—an addition by Megan's father. Tom Whittlebee had always had a bit of a bizarre side; Megan's mother affectionately referred to it as "The Whittlebee Weirdness."

Nevertheless, in Megan's mind, her house was the finest house in all of Shadyville, and it had always lifted her spirits when she caught sight of it. But not today, Megan thought with a frown. All she could think about was soon the house wouldn't be hers anymore.

As Megan got closer, she noticed her father's purple Volkswagen Beetle in the driveway. It was his last day of work as well, but he wasn't expected home until 5:30 pm.

Maybe he came home early to finish off that mangy cat across the street like he had always threatened to, Megan thought to herself and sniggered just before spying the wretched creature crouching at the base of a nearby tree, glaring at her with slanted, yellow eyes.

I wonder why it hates me so much, Megan thought, as she picked up a twig and threw it at the creature. The cat scampered up the tree and let out a menacing hiss through bared, pointed teeth. Megan glared back before entering the house.

Megan had expected to see her parents in the living room, packing her mother's bell collection and her father's jungle masks into boxes, but the room was empty. She took off her wet shoes and hung up her damp coat before climbing the stairs. At the top of the staircase, Megan heard her parents' hushed voices in the room at the end of the hall. It was her baby brother's room.

Oh no, Megan thought, *not Nicky!*

Nicholas Whittlebee had asthma, and someone always had to keep a close watch on him to make sure that he was all right. Megan had watched her parents put a plastic mask over Nicholas's face to administer his medicine countless times, and she had hated every second of it. Sometimes, when it got bad, Nicholas had to be taken to the hospital. Megan remembered all of this as she fearfully ran into her brother's room. Both of her parents turned to face her.

"Hey, Dodles," greeted her father with his usual quirky smile (Dodles was one of her father's many nicknames for her).

"How was your last day at school, honey?" her mother asked.

Megan didn't answer. "What's wrong with Nicky?" she asked fearfully as she neared her brother's crib.

"It was nothing," responded her mother. "I thought Nicholas was looking a little *off* so I took him to the hospital. The doctors assured us that he was fine."

Megan wasn't completely convinced; she thought her mother looked a little shook-up. Megan had opened her mouth to say so when her father put his hands on her shoulders and quickly ushered her out of the room and down the hall towards her own bedroom.

"I think your mother's a little nervous about the trip," Megan's father whispered to her. He grabbed a foam basketball and threw it through the hoop on the back of her door.

"So, how *did* school go today?" Megan's father repeated as he fell onto her bed, squashing about a dozen stuffed animals in the process.

"Fine," Megan lied as she turned away and pretended to look through the contents of her bag. What she had

The Charm Tree

really wanted to say was that Kendra and her group had left her a going away gift in the form of chocolate pudding on her chair at lunch. Megan had spent twenty-five minutes in the washroom trying to get it out of her blue jeans.

"Saying goodbye to all of your friends, I imagine," her father went on as he inspected a rather fat creature with purple horns and an orange belly, apparently trying to figure out what it was.

"Mmnn," Megan replied. In reality, she didn't have that many friends to say goodbye to. She had often spent her free time at school off in a corner by herself, losing herself in one of her fantasy books.

"You should try to look at this move as an exciting adventure, Cookie Crumb!" her father said enthusiastically as he moved to the side of the bed. "I had the greatest time in Shansymoon when I was a kid. One time, the guys and I hijacked a hot-air balloon and floated all over British Columbia. The balloon had a big smiley face on it, and we named it Mr. Fathead."

"Sure, Mr. Fathead," Megan replied dryly.

Megan's father went on excitedly, "We were going to fly the balloon to Spain to watch the bullfights, but a huge, purple bird flew into it and popped it with its beak. We all came crashing down into a giant spruce tree!"

"That's tragic," Megan commented without emotion as she started pulling liquorice and old gym socks from her bag.

"Yeah," Megan's father added with genuine regret in his voice.

Tom Whittlebee was always telling his daughter crazy stories about his childhood home. Shansymoon Creek was the place Megan's family was moving to. It was close to the mountains in northern British Columbia, and the creek, which ran around the outskirts of the town, was a tributary of the river Prophet. Shansymoon was a theatre town, and Megan's father had gotten a job as Manager of the main theatre, Mavilyn Theatre.

Megan didn't believe half of her father's tales about Shansymoon and the mountains, but they usually made her laugh. Not today, however. She just wasn't in the mood. Megan didn't like living in Shadyville, Ontario, but she didn't want to move all the way to British Columbia either. With a grimace, Megan pulled out a sticky, blue candy from the bottom of her backpack. In frustration she quickly threw it back in.

Megan's father sighed and took a silver chain off from around his neck. A clear, crystal trinket in the shape of a teardrop dangled from it, and for as long as Megan could remember, her father had always worn it.

The Charm Tree

"You know, Megan, one Christmas, when I was a boy, I was walking along a river up in the mountains, and I saw something shining out from the water. I walked over and looked down, and this is what I saw." He dangled the trinket in the light from Megan's bedside lamp, causing it to sparkle brilliantly and cast refractions of light around the room.

Megan's father went on, almost in a whisper, "I picked it up and put it in my pocket. That was when I saw, lying in the snow on the riverbank a short distance away, the figure of a tiny woman, no bigger than my hand. She had silver hair and translucent wings, which glittered in the sunlight, and one of her wings appeared to be damaged. I had never seen anything like her in my life. She even looked up at me; she had the saddest eyes I had ever seen."

Megan looked at the trinket, then at her father with growing interest. She had never seen that look in her father's eyes before.

He continued, "I ran to get my friends, who were having a snowball fight nearby, but when we got back to the spot, she was gone; there was no trace of her. No one believed me, of course, but I often went back into the mountains to look for her. I never saw her again."

Megan's father turned to her and gently placed the crystal in her hand. "Here's to your own adventures," he said with a twinkle in his eye.

Megan looked down at the trinket, which now glittered in her hand, with awe. Could the story have been true?

Megan's father scanned the room and took in the numerous half-filled boxes and piles of books and clothes covering the floor.

"You'd better finish packing, Carrot Cap, or we'll be leaving you behind to deal with that crazy cat that lives across the street. They say he's got eyes that can see right through you and fleas that will chew your skin off!" With a sly glint in his eye, Megan's father moved his hands close to her lamp and created a dark, shadowy shape that crept along the wall and seemed to come after her with huge, jagged jaws. Megan screamed with terrified delight.

Her father threw a stuffed tiger at her before jumping up to leave.

"I'll meet you in the dining room at 6:00," he added with a wink and a smile before sweeping out of the room and closing the door behind him.

Megan walked over to the window and looked out. The overcast sky left the view of the street below a colourless, murky grey—hopelessly uninviting. Megan caught sight of Kendra and her group walking down the

The Charm Tree

street under their umbrellas, and she immediately shrank back from the window. From her vantage point, Megan could see the dirty cat in the tree outside of her window, its tail swishing slowly and its fierce, yellow eyes fixated on the girls that were slowly moving towards it.

"Release your army of fleas upon my enemies," Megan whispered and giggled to herself.

Megan looked back at the trinket in her hand, and her feeling of awe began to melt. It had just been another absurd story that her father had made up to amuse her, she told herself. After all, there were no such things as tiny women with wings. Megan wrinkled her nose. And as for adventures, she thought they were highly overrated.

"I don't need them, and I don't want them!" Megan muttered to herself as she pushed the chain and crystal deep into her overstuffed suitcase. A moment later, however, Megan was struck with a pang of guilt and began to rummage through her suitcase for the chain. She was even more regretful when it took her twenty minutes to locate it in her jumble of stuff.

Megan put the chain around her neck and dropped it inside of her sweater. With a deep sigh, she stood up and gazed around her room at the many things that still needed to be packed. If only packing were the least of her worries, Megan thought as she remembered the move, and the terrible black puddle began to bubble up in her stomach again.

That night, Megan dreamed. She could see something up ahead, shining like silver in the moonlight, and Megan was filled with the desire to run towards it. As she did so, the surrounding trees and undergrowth began to snag her clothes, and the large roots made her stumble. Megan knew that if she could just get to the silver light, everything would be all right, but the more she ran, the more distant the light seemed to become.

Suddenly frightened, Megan faltered and looked wildly about her. Darkness was creeping through the forest, and a cold wind picked up, sending a chill through her body. Megan's heart began to beat loudly in her ears as she sensed danger lurking in the shadows. The swaying branches were closing in on her like gnarled fingers, blocking out the light of the twinkling stars overhead. The air—crisp and clean just minutes before—was now thin and too close.

Megan gasped and wheezed as she felt the skeletal branches tighten around her chest. She tried to scream out, but her throat had become constricted and could not take in air. Megan clawed madly at the branches like a wild animal caught in a trap, but it was no use; she wasn't

The Charm Tree

strong enough to free herself from their icy clutches. Panic overwhelmed Megan's senses as the darkness swam in around her...

Megan bolted up in bed, wheezing and gasping through terrified sobs. Her room was pitch black, and the darkness seemed to constrain her like a blanket that had been tucked in too tightly. After a few moments, Megan began to perceive her surroundings, and her heartbeat and breathing began to slow. Immediately, Megan's thoughts flew to her brother Nicholas in his crib down the hall. She knew something was wrong.

In a flash, Megan was out the door and running down the hall. Once in her brother's room, she flicked on the light switch and ran to his crib. Nicholas's eyes were closed, and he was squirming under his blankets. His face was very pale and damp, and his chest was heaving. Every wheezing gasp sent a chill down Megan's spine.

Megan screamed for her parents and ran to their room next door with her heart in her throat, and within a few moments they were all at the side of Nicholas's crib. Megan's mother fearfully scooped up her son into her arms as Megan's father ran for the phone.

After a terrifying fifteen minutes in which Megan had huddled in the corner of her brother's room, clutching her queasy stomach as she watched her mother hold the plastic mask over Nicholas's face, the ambulance arrived.

Megan was left with their neighbour Mrs. Everly while her parents went with Nicholas to the hospital. Megan had desperately wanted to go with her family, but her father assured her that they would be back soon.

"We'll all be back and snug as a bug in a rug before you know it, French Fry," he quickly uttered before jumping into the back of the ambulance. Megan had never seen her father look so scared.

Mrs. Everly took Megan into her kitchen and kindly offered her a cup of hot chocolate. She was a sweet, old lady with long, white hair and huge glasses, who often gave Megan cookies and let her play in her backyard. Even though Mrs. Everly's eyes were filled with concern, she tried to smile at Megan as she brought over the steaming cup.

"Babies get sick all the time, dear," she said. "Nicholas will be back soon, you'll see."

Megan found she couldn't speak, but to please her kind neighbour she took the cup of hot chocolate and drank it down. The hot, sweet liquid helped to ease the dark and empty feeling in Megan's stomach.

When Megan had finished, Mrs. Everly led her to the living room, where she told her to lie down on the sofa. Then she covered Megan with a brown afghan.

"You just rest now," Mrs. Everly said softly. "I'll be sure to wake you when I hear some news."

The Charm Tree

Megan felt numb. She wanted to believe that it was all a horrible nightmare and that she would wake up soon. For hours she lay awake, staring at the shaded swirls on the ceiling and listening for the telephone to ring. Eventually, Megan dozed off, but she had a very fitful sleep.

Megan awoke to the sensation of something rubbing her shoulder, and when she opened her eyes, she perceived pale light streaming in through the large, living room window. Megan's father was standing over her, looking very tired but happy.

"Nicky's okay," he said as Megan fell into his arms, brilliant relief flooding through her. "The doctors were able to take care of him, and we should be able to bring him home later today."

Mrs. Everly clapped her hands and held them under her chin with suppressed emotion. "I just knew that baby boy would pull through," she said, her eyes tearing under her large glasses.

As Megan's father carried her home over the early morning dew, a tear slid down her cheek. She wished deep in her heart that she would never have to go through another frightening night like this. Drained by fatigue and emotion, Megan failed to notice the crystal trinket around her neck, which had begun to glow with the faintest of light…

★ 2 ★
The Big Move

It was Friday, and Megan awoke to brilliant sunlight shining in her eyes. It was already late morning. Megan caught the delicious scent of frying bacon as she raced down the stairs and into the kitchen. Her father was standing at the stove in bright orange pajamas spotted with green alligators.

"Is Nicky back?" Megan asked eagerly.

"Hold your horses, Pumpkin Face, and set the table," her father responded as he cracked an egg into a sizzling pan. "Your mother stayed at the hospital last night, and she just called to say that we can go over to pick them both up."

Megan was ecstatic. She quickly gobbled down her food before running back upstairs to throw on a pair of jeans and a sweater. Her father's loud voice trailed after her. "Don't forget your brother's green—er—frog!" he yelled. "He can't be without it!"

Soon afterwards, Megan and her father were in their purple Beetle and on their way to the hospital. Megan was clutching her brother's favourite green bunny in her arms. One of its ears was nearly ripped off, and it seemed to be missing half of its whiskers, but Nicholas loved the wretched toy more than anything.

Nicholas was happy to see Megan and his green bunny. He grabbed hold of it and began chewing on its ear as Megan helped the nurse dress him into his winter suit. As Megan leaned over, the crystal trinket fell out of her sweater and dangled above Nicholas, shining brightly in the late morning sun. Nicholas's eyes opened wide, and he dropped his bunny, letting it tumble to the floor. He eagerly reached for the shining object, but Megan threw it back into her sweater hastily. She knew how much Nicholas had liked to pull on the trinket when it had been hanging from her father's neck, and she didn't particularly want red marks on her neck from the chain cutting in. Nicholas squeezed Megan's fingers and kicked his legs joyously. Megan smiled back and kissed her brother twice on his chubby cheeks.

Megan's parents had some final words with the doctor, and soon enough the Whittlebees were all in the car and

The Charm Tree

on their way home. Mrs. Everly waved at them from her living room window as the Whittlebees pulled into their driveway. Nicholas waved his green bunny at her in return. After a kiss for both Megan and Nicholas, their sleepy mother went up to bed for a nap.

"Doodle Bug, you and I have a big job ahead of us," Megan's father said to her. "Let's get the living room packed before your mother wakes up—a banana split with olives to the one who can fill the most boxes!"

Nicholas was placed in a playpen nearby, where Megan and her father could keep a close eye on him. He gurgled and blew bubbles as he sat on his bunny and oversaw the proceedings. Soon, the living room was packed, and Megan moved upstairs to finish up in her bedroom.

She had been told to pack two suitcases to last for a month or two. The Whittlebees' belongings would be placed in storage in Shansymoon Creek, and the family would be staying with Megan's aunt and uncle while her parents searched for a house of their own.

Megan had remembered visiting her aunt and uncle only once when she was five years old. They had a son her age named Blaise, who had freckles and messy, blonde hair. Megan remembered with a groan how her cousin had put sand down the back of her pants before pushing her into a mud pit. She wasn't looking forward to the reunion.

Megan's suitcases filled up quickly, and she found it difficult to decide what was of utmost importance to take with her. Though she was in grade six, Megan was still very attached to her stuffed animals. She couldn't stand the thought of her large, white teddy bear Mortimer being packed away in a box for months, so she tried to fit him into an overstuffed suitcase amongst a confused heap of jeans, sweaters and books.

In two days time the moving trucks would be arriving, and Megan's family would be driving to Ottawa to catch their flight to British Columbia. Megan had never flown before, and the thought of it filled her with more than a little trepidation. When she had voiced her fear to her parents, her father had offered to fly the family to Shansymoon Creek in a rocket ship he had been working on in the garage. Megan had quickly decided that an airplane might not be so bad after all.

When Megan had finished packing up her room, she went downstairs and played with Nicholas, while her father went out to finish packing up the things in the garage. She looked over at the living room wall, where a purple mouse with a three-foot long, curling tail sat peering back at her oddly with its red eyes. Megan had drawn the creature with crayons and lipstick when she was three, and her father had never let her mother wash

The Charm Tree

it off. He had declared that it was a fine work of art, and he showed it off to all of his guests with pride.

Vivid visions of piggy-back rides, shadow puppets and laugh attacks that almost made her pee her pants flashed through Megan's mind before slowly melting away, bringing Megan back into the present. Now the house looked strange and hollow with everything in boxes. Even the sounds were amplified in the vast emptiness. Megan didn't like the feeling at all. She picked up her brother and held him close, attempting to fill the cold emptiness that had begun to creep through her slowly.

The next day, men from a vehicle shipping company came to pick up the Whittlebees' purple Beetle, and on Sunday morning, the movers arrived to pack their furniture and boxes into a large truck. While two of the movers were sniggering and pointing at Tom Whittlebee's giant, ceramic, pink and yellow snail with bulging eyes, which Mrs. Whittlebee had left in the front yard ("as a house warming gift for the new owners!" she had explained earnestly), Megan said goodbye to her beloved house and yard. Then she and her family piled into a rental van.

With tears in her eyes, Mrs. Everly brought over a tin of homemade Nanaimo bars—Megan's favourite—and wished the family a safe trip. Even the dirty cat from across the street appeared to give them one final spat as the Whittlebees drove down their street for the last time.

Hot tears came to Megan's eyes as she looked back, watching the scene until the van turned a corner, and her house and kind neighbor vanished from sight. She resented the new family that would soon be moving in, sleeping in her room and wiping away her purple mouse. She wished them evil cat scratches and chocolate pudding on their seats.

During the road trip to Ottawa, Megan's father attempted to amuse everyone with stories of a strange man named Johnny Rodriguez, a fierce and noble warrior, who wielded a deadly knife and battled his archenemy Frank de Loop for the favour of the fair Jezebel. Megan was in a sour mood, but she couldn't help but wonder what it would be like to be Jezebel, in bright flowing gowns, with two handsome men fighting over her. She began to imagine herself riding a white stallion under a starry sky with the wind blowing through her hair as she returned to her beautiful home with cool gardens and large water fountains.

"It might not be so bad, huh?" she whispered to Nicholas, who was banging his bunny against the side of his car seat excitedly. Megan sighed, "But it's not my life," she whispered as she leaned her forehead against the

The Charm Tree

cold glass of the van window and watched the scenery passing by.

A few hours later, the Whittlebees arrived at the Ottawa International Airport. They had to stand in a long line to get their tickets, and the wait at the gate for their boarding call seemed to take forever. Megan glared at all of the little children who were running around, playing and screaming and rubbing at their wet noses. They seemed to be swarming around the Whittlebees as Megan's father started making funny faces and pulling tiny, rubber dinosaurs out from behind the ears of each child. From his mother's lap, Nicholas was laughing and clapping his hands with excitement.

When the Whittlebees were finally seated on the plane, Megan started to feel anxious again about the flight. She was glad to be seated next to the window so that she could see out at least. As the engines started up and the plane began to move, Megan could see and hear flaps opening up on the wings. The plane slowly drove down the runway before halting momentarily. Megan grabbed onto her armrests fearfully and braced herself when the plane started moving and quickly gaining in speed. When the plane lifted off the ground and began to ascend, Megan gasped as she felt pulled into the back of her seat. Her mother gave her a bubble gum ball to chew to relieve the pressure she began to feel building in her ears. Megan squeezed her eyes shut and tried to imagine happy things, like large, silvery fish swimming through a sunny sky.

When nothing at all resembling a disaster happened, Megan's fear began to lessen somewhat. She opened her eyes and looked down at the view from her window. She was mesmerized by how quickly the roads and buildings beneath her became thin lines and tiny squares. As the plane entered the clouds, Megan couldn't help but feel that she was completely surrounded by white cotton candy, and once above the clouds, she found herself in a brilliant, blue sky with a sunlit floor of white fluff that seemed to go on forever. Megan had often lain in the grass, gazing up into the sky, and wondered what it would be like to be on top of the clouds. Now she knew!

Once the Flight Attendants had brought out the drinks and meals, and Megan had settled down to watch the featured movie, she began to feel that flying wasn't so bad. In fact, halfway through the romantic comedy, she began to feel so comfortable that she dozed off. Hours later, Megan awoke to a message over the plane's intercom stating that they were beginning their descent into Vancouver International Airport. Megan looked out of her window excitedly and was amazed to see the large British Columbia city sprawled out beneath her.

The Charm Tree

Megan's father leaned over and whispered to her, "We'll bring you back here in the spring. Vancouver is a fascinating city with so much to see and do. But today, we'll need to catch a flight to Fort St. John and then on to Fort Nelson up north.

A little of Megan's fear returned when the plane finally hit the runway with a loud bounce, and she was once more pushed into the back of her seat as the plane sped down the runway. Nicholas smiled and clutched at her sweater sleeve from his father's lap, and Megan felt a warm surge flow through her. Her baby brother didn't seem to be afraid of anything.

Once off of the plane, the Whittlebees had just enough time to catch a quick bite to eat at the airport and then run to catch their next flight to Fort St. John. Megan's mother explained that this trip would only take an hour and a half. Megan thought that didn't sound so bad compared to the five-hour flight from Ottawa to Vancouver. However, Megan was pleasantly surprised that it was three hours earlier in British Columbia than it was in Ontario, and she had to change her watch.

"It's like our trip to Vancouver only took two hours!" Megan's father said enthusiastically. It had indeed felt that way to Megan as she had slept for most of the trip. But now she was well rested, and once seated on the second plane, she wrapped herself up cozily in a blanket that one of the Flight Attendants had given her, and she pulled out a book from her carry-on bag. When the plane started moving down the runway and gaining in speed, Megan merely shot her brother a quick wink and kept reading her book until they were high in the sky again. She wasn't going to feel frightened this time.

Soon enough, Megan was lost in a misty world of magical sorcerers and axe-wielding dwarves. When she looked out her window at the magnificent, white, jagged peaks of the Rocky Mountains beneath her, it was easy to imagine herself in that place, mining for jewels in the depths of the mountains or shooting enchanted arrows at enemies in the forest. Megan would have given anything to be in that magical world and leave her own dreary world behind.

It seemed like only moments later that Megan was pulled from a dangerous confrontation with a nasty, drooling troll, as she heard a message over the intercom stating that the plane was nearing the North Peace Regional Airport in Fort St. John.

"Sorry, honey, but we do have one more flight to catch," Megan's mother explained wearily as Megan helped her to gather up all of Nicholas's toys that had become strewn about. Nicholas's usual sunny demeanor was being tested with all of the travelling. He was beginning to get fussy and difficult to manage.

The Charm Tree

"Gum Drop, put on your coat and hat once we land," Megan's father said. "It'll be cold outside."

Megan looked out of her window at the white land beneath her. Though it was November, Shadyville had only experienced cold rain showers, but here, snow covered the ground. Once the plane landed, Megan grabbed her things and followed her mother down the staircase that had been pulled down from the plane. The sun was low in the sky, and Megan felt a shiver run through her. She wasn't sure if it was due to the cool wind that now whipped around her or the strange sensation of being in a new land far from her home. She pulled the hood of her green parka up over her head to provide some protection from the cold that was now creeping around her as well as through her.

Megan and her family made their way into the airport to await their next flight to Fort Nelson. They quickly found a café, where they ordered some hot drinks. As Megan was sipping her hot chocolate with whipped cream, her mother reminded her to use the airport washroom before they had to board the next plane. Megan stood up and started to make her way to the washroom. However, before she could take two steps, a rather large man carrying a tray of food bumped into her accidentally, sending her crashing into a redheaded girl, who was sitting at a nearby table. The girl let out a shrill cry as the pop she had been drinking spilt down her green blouse. She shot Megan a look of pure venom as Megan apologized hastily and quickly crossed the café.

Megan decided to spend some extra time in the washroom, cleaning her hands thoroughly and playing with her unruly, auburn hair. When she finally returned to her table, she was careful not to make eye contact with the redheaded girl as she finished her now only lukewarm drink.

Soon it was time for the Whittlebees to board their third and last plane of the trip. The sun was setting as the family left the airport and made their way over to the small plane. Once onboard, Megan found their seats halfway down the plane, and she sat down next to the window. Her mother and Nicholas sat down beside her while her father sat across the aisle, already entrenched in a local newspaper.

Megan grabbed a couple of toys out of her mother's carry-on bag to amuse Nicholas with. She was just in the process of blowing loud zerberts on her brother's belly, causing him to giggle and kick his legs, when Megan heard shrill laughter. She looked up and saw the girl that she had bumped into in the airport standing in the aisle, pointing at her and laughing hysterically. Megan could feel her face flush immediately, and she sat back in her chair and waited for the girl to pass. She was glad that

The Charm Tree

this was going to be a very short flight, and she pulled out her book, planning to lose herself once more in another place and time.

Just a few minutes later, however, Megan heard giggling coming from the seats behind her, followed by the sensation of jarring jabs in her back. As she peaked over the back of her seat gingerly, Megan saw a small boy with red hair, smiling at her obnoxiously and kicking her seat, and the girl with the soiled blouse was sitting next to him. She shot Megan a smug grin. Megan wished her mother could do something about these evil children, but at the moment, her mother was busily attempting to keep a squirming and cranky Nicholas in her arms.

Once the plane was in the air, and Megan was still trying to ignore the assault from behind, she sighed deeply and looked out at the darkening sky. Even on a small plane in what seemed to be the middle of nowhere, trouble seemed to find her. Nicholas was now crying loudly and hurling whatever toys his parents tried to appease him with, and just as Megan felt that her situation couldn't get much worse, the older man seated in front of her lowered his seat so far back that Megan began to feel like she was trapped inside of a sandwich that bit back!

Though this last flight lasted less than an hour, Megan felt that it took a lifetime for the plane to reach Fort Nelson. Upon arrival, Megan tried to rush her parents off of the plane and into the airport, and she was careful to avoid looking in the direction of the redheaded children, whom she was beginning to suspect had horns and spiked tails concealed on their bodies.

The Whittlebees didn't have trouble finding their luggage on the conveyor belt in the airport, as most of it was bright orange with funny stickers plastered all over it. The travel bags, proudly purchased by Megan's father, had always seemed to be a slight cause of embarrassment for her mother when they traveled, and she seemed anxious to hide them away in the trunk of the taxi. After a brief spell of confusion over who would sit where, the Whittlebees were off on the short drive to Shansymoon Creek.

As they entered the town and drove down the narrow streets, Megan noticed differences from her old town immediately. Under the golden light of the street lamps walked people who were dressed in funny clothes, such as ball gowns, beanie caps and brightly-coloured tights. Dogs and cats seemed to be running loose with abandon, and as the taxi stopped at an intersection, Megan spotted a parrot perched atop a snow-covered signpost. She rolled down her window to get a better look.

"Where you wanna go?" the parrot squawked.

Before Megan could answer, the taxi turned down the main street of Shansymoon, and several shops with interesting costumes in the windows came into view.

The Charm Tree

"This is an *art*sy town," her mother whispered to her. Megan couldn't help but be interested in the wondrous sights from her window.

At the end of the main street was a park surrounded by a black, iron fence. There were tall trees and bushes within the fence, blowing in the wind, but as the taxi passed by a large gateway, Megan caught a glimpse of a huge, dark building in the centre of the park. It reminded her of a castle she had once seen in one of her books. An ornate sign over the gate read *Mavilyn Theatre*.

"There's my new workplace," Megan's father declared proudly. He looked over at the large building wistfully. "I can remember the oddest things happening in that theatre when I was a boy: strange noises and moving shadows where there should have been only sets and dusty props." Megan's father looked at her meaningfully before grabbing her and crying, "Boo!" Megan screamed out and giggled as her father tickled her.

"My brother and his wife Dolly live just around the corner, and your new school is just a fifteen-minute walk from their house, Cherry Snout," Megan's father said as he put an arm around her. "You'll be able to walk with your cousin."

At the mention of her new school *and* her cousin, dark butterflies fluttered into Megan's stomach. She had tried, rather unsuccessfully, to push these thoughts from her mind since the onset of the trip.

As the taxi rounded a corner, Megan spotted a bright yellow sign that read *Snicker Doodle*. This seemed to be a very opulent street; the houses were large and grand and had huge front yards. They weren't quaint and cozy like Megan's old house in Shadyville; however, she couldn't help but feel impressed.

The taxi drove almost to the end of the street and pulled up in front of an odd-looking house with apple-green siding and orange shutters that didn't quite seem to fit in with the rest of the homes on the street. The yard was a tad overgrown, and there was a bike and skateboard sticking out of the snow on the lawn. The garage door was half open, revealing an extremely cluttered and messy interior. Megan's mother had always liked things to be trim and tidy, and Megan couldn't help but notice her eyes widen at the sight.

As the Whittlebees started unpacking their luggage from the trunk of the taxi, a short and rather wide woman with very curly brown hair came bounding down the front steps of the house to greet them. She was wearing brown slacks and red flip-flop shoes. Her chins jiggled as she chortled and clapped her hands.

"You're here, you're here!" she cried out joyously

The Charm Tree

"Dolly!" exclaimed Megan's father. "It's great to see you. You're looking as lovely as a springtime cherry blossom," he said as he gave her a warm hug.

"Oh, Tom, you always were a smooth talker," Dolly replied with a hearty chuckle before kissing Megan's mother on the cheek and greeting Nicholas excitedly. When the bubbly woman glimpsed Megan, still standing shyly near the trunk of the taxi, she bulged out her huge chest with glee.

"Oooh, and this must be little Megan!" Dolly declared breathlessly as she tottered over to Megan and pulled her into a tight embrace. Megan found herself getting lost in her aunt's enormous, fleshy body. "But I guess you're not so little any more, are you? I wager you'll grow up to be a tall beauty just like your mother," Dolly exclaimed and squeezed Megan's cheeks with her pudgy fingers.

Presently, a thin man emerged from the house, followed by a boy with freckles and long, disheveled, blonde hair. Megan knew that this must be her Uncle George and cousin Blaise. The man was tall, like Megan's father, and she noticed that he had the same nose. He wore a dark green sweater vest and faded, black cords. Blaise stood near him with his arms folded over his T-shirt, and he looked at Megan curiously, while the bottoms of his oversized jeans got wet in the snow. A mischievous glint flashed in his eyes, and Megan had the sudden vision of herself being picked up and thrown into a snow bank.

The tall man approached Megan and loomed over her. "Welcome to Shansymoon—the place where peculiar things happen at every turn and tick of the clock," he uttered in a guttural voice. Megan felt her skin tingle at his intense words and presence, and she shrank back towards the taxi.

"Don't scare the poor girl, George," Dolly said with a chuckle. "Well, let's not stand out here in the cold all day," she exclaimed excitedly. "My toes will positively turn blue and fall off! Let's go inside."

They all entered the house and left the luggage and coats in the foyer. Uncle George led Megan's family into a cluttered living room with plush, orange carpet and gold-papered walls. Megan sank deeply into a white, plastic chair that was shaped like an egg and quietly watched the adults catch up on news and happenings. Aunt Dolly was absolutely cooing over Nicholas, while Blaise sat on the floor and absent-mindedly poked at a large turtle he called Gertie Pertrude.

Megan gazed around the oddly-decorated room and spotted a photo of two grinning boys, whom she suspected to be her father and Uncle George when they were younger. Megan gasped as she saw what appeared to

The Charm Tree

be the remains of a bright yellow hot air balloon behind them.

Suddenly, her Aunt Dolly pulled Megan up and out of her chair mercilessly.

"Suppertime, Cutie!" She cried and giggled.

"Perfect," Megan murmured unenthusiastically as she rubbed her sore shoulder.

Everyone moved into the dining room for dinner. Megan noticed numerous portraits on the gold and green-papered walls depicting Blaise at various ages. In every photo he looked unkempt and had a peculiar expression on his face. Megan snorted into her hand when she caught sight of a portrait of Blaise with a nasty scowl and a large, green stain on his T-shirt. Blaise followed her gaze and sat up straighter with pride.

"I haven't smiled in a single one yet!" he declared triumphantly before proceeding to violently smoosh his peas into his mashed potatoes and squeeze a mountain of mustard on top. Nicholas watched interestedly from his highchair before squishing his peas between his hands earnestly.

Uncle George was a professor of Metaphysics at the local college, and throughout dinner he talked about his classes and students. "Can you believe that one of my students tried to convince me that deadlines for assignments should be obsolete? His argument was that only the present time exists, so future deadlines are an illusion. I told him that in that case, he'd better get his assignment on my desk right now. He sure changed his tune quick!" Uncle George hit the table and howled with laughter at his own story before muttering, "Now, what did I do with my fork…?"

Megan learned that her Aunt Dolly was a self-employed craftswoman, who sold her wares at the local market. Giggling, her aunt pointed to the buffet, where a thingamabob made of pipe cleaners and bottle caps teetered precariously.

"Oh, it's great," Megan declared weakly as she tried in vain to figure out what it was.

After rice pudding, Aunt Dolly suggested that Blaise show Megan to her room.

"Aw, Mom," complained Blaise, "I told Jared that I would come over after dinner to check out his new Star Car Racer game."

"That's perfect!" declared Aunt Dolly happily (Megan noticed that her aunt seemed to get excited over the littlest things). "You can take Megan with you and introduce her to Jared's sister."

"Jared and Helena are the grandchildren of Sadie Mavilyn, your new employer," Uncle George explained to Megan's father. "They live just down the street, as I expect you remember."

The Charm Tree

"Twins, you know," Aunt Dolly added as she winked at Megan.

Megan wasn't sure she felt up to meeting new people just yet. She shot a desperate look at her mother, who gave her shoulder a gentle squeeze.

"Go on, Megan," she said encouragingly, "it will be nice for you to meet some people before you start school."

Megan got up and followed her cousin from the room reluctantly. In a way, she was almost glad to escape the incessant, bubbly chatter of her Aunt Dolly.

★ 3 ★
Meeting the Mavilyns

Blaise led Megan back through the living room and into the foyer, where they grabbed their jackets. Blaise put on enormous, black boots and slipped on a blue and purple toque that reached far down his back. They went out into the cold evening and started walking towards the very end of Snicker Doodle Street.

"I don't know why you would want to meet Helena," Blaise said as he tramped along in his untied boots. "She's such a bore she makes me snore. But Jared's pretty cool, and they've got a wicked house!" he added as he kicked some powdery snow into the air. Megan watched her cousin uneasily out of the corner of her eye, not quite sure what to make of him. She had the feeling that he might do something outrageous at any moment, like the evening, long ago, when he had howled loudly for fifteen minutes straight until he had every dog in the neighbourhood answering back.

"Whittlebee Weirdness," Megan muttered to herself.

"What?" Blaise asked as he threw the end of his toque over his shoulder.

"Oh—er—I said—little pixies are beardless!" Megan replied lamely.

Blaise shot her a sidewise glance that made her feel like a deranged madwoman. Megan felt like pulling her brown, knit toque down over her face.

Just a few houses down from Blaise's house, a huge mansion of grey stone loomed up, and it momentarily took Megan's breath away. Shiny brass numbers on the open, iron fence read "111". Blaise and Megan followed the half-moon driveway to the large front steps, where two extremely ugly and menacing gargoyles—one smiling and one frowning—guarded the way. Megan blanched momentarily when she saw them.

"I know, they're pretty freaky!" Blaise declared happily as he patted one affectionately on the snout.

Though the large, oak doors were adorned with ornate, brass knockers, Blaise found, beside the left door, what looked like a gnarled and taloned hand with the index finger pointing outwards as if to warn visitors to go away. Blaise grabbed hold of the finger and pulled down.

The Charm Tree

A funny sound like a loud *boing!* and then a whistling *zip!* reverberated throughout the house. Megan started to laugh, but she had to quickly cover her mouth, as presently, the door opened to reveal a short and somewhat plump man with chubby cheeks. He was dressed in tails and seemed to look down upon the children with distaste.

"Mr. Whittlebee," greeted the man in a dry voice. "Mrs. Mavilyn and her grandchildren are currently at dinner."

"Step aside, Baxter!" Blaise ordered, trying to look important as he puffed out his chest (Megan thought her cousin looked rather funny with his torn jacket and ludicrously long toque). "I have important business here with Jared."

Before the disgruntled butler could reply, Blaise had grabbed Megan and pulled her past him, drawing her into a grand foyer. Megan barely had a chance to look at her surroundings before Blaise had dragged her past some scarlet, velvet hangings, which opened into an opulent dining room. There, sitting at a large, circular table, was an older woman in a black, frilly dress with her hair pinned up in loose curls. She had a child on either side of her.

"Blaise!" called the woman. "How good of you to join us; we're just having dessert. Do come in with your friend and sit down." The two children sitting beside the woman looked at Megan interestedly.

Megan sat down beside a girl with long, dark hair and brown eyes. She was wearing a purple, velvet dress, and Megan couldn't help but notice that she appeared to have a glass of red wine in front of her. Blaise walked around the table to sit beside a boy with short hair, as dark as the girl's, but Megan noticed that the boy had darker skin. He was wearing a neat, black shirt that was buttoned up to the collar. There were two silver platters on the table: one filled with fruit, and the other, to Megan's surprise, was filled with gummy worms.

"Why don't you introduce us to your friend, Blaise?" prompted the woman, smiling. Megan thought the woman's voice sounded crackly but not altogether unpleasant.

"Oh, this is Megan Whittlebee, my cousin," Blaise answered offhandedly as he helped himself to a few worms. "Her family is staying with us until they find their own place," he mumbled with his mouth full of goo.

"Splendid!" replied the woman with a clap of her hands. "Well then, you must be Tom's daughter."

Megan gave a weak nod as the girl beside her flipped her hair over her shoulder dramatically and peered at Megan curiously.

The Charm Tree

"I was extremely displeased when your father left Shansymoon all those years ago," the woman went on, "and I racked my brain for a way to tempt him back. I just knew that my theatre would do the trick. Yes, little Tommy used to love racing through the theatre's echoing corridors and hiding in its shadowy corners. Once a Shansymooner, always a Shansymooner, I say. My name is Sadie Mavilyn, and these are my grandchildren, Jared and Helena."

Megan nodded politely. The girl sitting beside her gave an audible sniff.

"Nobody comes to Shansymoon unless they're dragged here," she said in a rather haughty voice as she picked up her glass and began to sip its contents regally. Megan suddenly had unpleasant visions of another Kendra Karson.

"Come now, Helena," replied Mrs. Mavilyn, "Shansymoon Creek is the finest town in all of Canada. The most fascinating people live here, and we do throw the best parties."

"And we have an awesome festival that comes to the theatre grounds every spring!" added Jared enthusiastically.

Megan caught sight of Blaise and chuckled into her hand. He had two green gummy worms hanging from his nostrils and was in the process of inserting two orange ones into his ears.

"Ugh!" cried Helena. "You're so uncivilized, Blaise," she spat before picking up a pear and throwing it at Blaise's head. She hit him square on the forehead. Blaise snorted, and one of the green gummies landed in Jared's milk. The other one flew across the table and fell into Baxter's evening jacket, while he was in the process of filling Megan's cup with milk.

"Good shot, Helena!" bellowed Mrs. Mavilyn, pounding her fist on the table. "Why, if you didn't spend all of your time at those ballet lessons, I think I might consider signing you up for baseball next summer."

"Ha!" Blaise exclaimed with contempt. "Helena wouldn't be caught dead in a baseball uniform. It wouldn't have enough *frills and lace*," he added derisively.

Blaise had to duck quickly to escape getting beaned on the nose with an apple.

"Well, Baxter," Mrs. Mavilyn muttered as she slowly rose from the table, "I think I'll take my nightcap early tonight. Yes, I think a nice shot of brandy will warm these old toes faster than any roaring fire can." She placed a hand on Jared's shoulder. "Children, why don't you give our new guest a tour of the house? I think she may find it interesting." Mrs. Mavilyn smiled at Megan before leaving

The Charm Tree

the room, followed by a very displeased butler. Megan decided she liked the older woman immensely.

"I'm rather fond of this table," Helena said sweetly as she offered Megan some strawberries. "It's an exact replica of King Arthur's table at Camelot."

"Don't be stupid, Helena," shot Jared. "Nobody knows what King Arthur's table really looked like."

"Grandmother says it's an exact replica, and I believe her!" Helena spat at her twin.

"Knock it off!" exclaimed Blaise. "I want to check out your new game, Jared."

"All right," Jared replied. "Let's show Megan the downstairs, and then Helena can take her upstairs."

"Since when do you tell me what to do?" Helena asked her twin with another flick of her long hair.

Megan looked at the other children with dismay and felt herself sinking down into her chair. She couldn't help but feel that she was a tad unwanted at the moment.

Helena changed her demeanor suddenly and smiled at the others. "Let's go, everyone," she said with a pleasant voice that Megan sensed was not altogether genuine.

As the children were getting up to leave the room, Megan whispered to Blaise, "Does Mrs. Mavilyn really let Helena drink wine?" she asked incredulously.

"It's just cranberry juice," Blaise whispered back, rolling his eyes and twirling his finger at his temple. "Helena's a loony."

The children passed through the draped doorway and re-entered the hall. As they crossed the expansive room, Megan noticed a large, blue-carpeted staircase leading up to a second floor, and as she looked up, Megan saw gold stars painted on the high, midnight blue ceiling.

"This house is amazing," Megan commented.

"Wait until you see the Roman bath," Jared replied with wide eyes. "Grandmother says that every room should be a world unto itself."

The children passed through a doorway at the other end of the hall that was draped with purple hangings that were covered with silver moons. Megan gasped upon first sight of the interior. Upon a hot pink couch sat a very manicured white poodle wagging its outrageous tail at the children. Balloons of every colour were scattered about, and in the corner of the room was a miniature carousel with four jaunty ponies prancing around and around to carnival music.

"This is the Carnival Room," Helena explained as she opened her arms wide to take in the wondrous scene.

Megan was delighted by what she saw. She passed by a panel of mirrors that distorted her reflection beyond recognition before noticing a life-size statue of a clown.

The Charm Tree

It was dressed in a blue and green-striped costume and had a sparkling, silver tear on its painted cheek. Megan reached up to touch the tear and screamed—the statue had turned its head and bit her.

"Got you!" it said and laughed boisterously as Megan fell back in surprise.

"Don't be frightened of him," said Helena. "That's Uncle Francis; he works at the theatre."

"Crazy loony," mumbled Blaise under his breath as he picked up a sparkling baton with bright, flowing tassels and threw it at the clown's shin.

"Hey, pull my finger!" cried Uncle Francis, who was clutching his injured leg and hopping up and down on the other, as the children quickly passed through the next set of doors into what appeared to be a medieval library. The moonlight pouring in through a high, glass-domed ceiling, along with a few torches and scantily-placed candles, provided the only illumination in the vast room. What seemed to be an infinite number of bound books reached to the ceiling, and a spiraling staircase led up to a second level. The children's footsteps echoed on the stone floor as they passed by wooden tables that held strange, metal contraptions. Megan thought the room was incredible. She couldn't help but wonder what secrets lay in the many books that lined the walls.

"I usually come here to do my homework and study," explained Jared, and when Helena was safely out of earshot, he leaned over and whispered to Megan, "It's a great place to escape my sister. She hates this room—too dusty and nothing but books." Megan looked up at Jared and smiled; she thought he had a kind face.

"You're welcome to take a closer look," Jared offered as he gestured towards the bookshelves, apparently reading Megan's mind.

Megan walked over to a shelf and began perusing the various titles: *Plato's Atlantis, Arabian Nights, The Seven Wonders of the Ancient World*...Megan thought the books looked very old and intriguing. Her hand stopped at a particularly attractive, leather-bound volume entitled *The Universe and the Beings Who Live There*. Megan pulled the book out and began flipping through it.

"All right, enough of this already!" said Blaise impatiently. "I didn't come here to look at dirty, old books. Come on, Jared, let's get out of here."

Megan gingerly placed the book she had been looking at on one of the wooden tables.

"Fine!" responded Helena with her nose in the air. "Come on, Megan, I'll show you the best room in the house," she said as she grabbed Megan's arm and began steering her back out of the library. Megan began to think that Helena was a snooty brat, and she didn't particularly

The Charm Tree

want to go with her, but she found herself being led away against her will.

The children went back through the Carnival Room and found Uncle Francis slouching on the pink sofa, puffing on a cigar, while his poodle gnawed viciously on one of the carousel pony's legs.

Once back in the hall, the children climbed the large, blue staircase. At the top, Helena led Megan down one corridor, while Jared and Blaise headed down another. As the girls walked, Megan snuck peeks into some of the rooms and was amazed by what she saw. One room was covered with bright carpets and dozens of fat pillows, and another room looked like an old-fashioned soda bar with a jukebox. Yet another room seemed to be shaped like a pyramid with strange designs painted on the walls. Megan wanted to stop and investigate each room, but Helena seemed determined to push on. Finally, the girls halted in front of two doors that were painted white and carved ornately with silver.

"This is my room," explained Helena proudly as she pushed open the doors dramatically. "I decorated it myself," she added with another flip of her hair.

As Megan stepped inside, she concluded immediately that it was just the sort of room she would have imagined a girl like Helena sleeping in. The carpet was white and so plush that Megan had to practically wade through it.

The walls were papered silver and mauve, and the large bed was covered with mauve hangings and silver tassels. The ceiling was painted with clouds and pastel colours to appear like the morning sky, and two glass doors opened out onto a small balcony that overlooked the garden.

In through those doors crept a sleek, black cat with a chewed-up piece of orange plastic in its mouth. The cat dropped the object—which looked somewhat like the mangled remains of a pocket protector—onto the carpet and sat up straight, swishing its tail proudly.

Helena walked over and shut the glass doors before the room could turn into an icebox.

"Who's this?" asked Megan as the cat came over to investigate her.

"That's Sapphire," answered Helena. She walked over and scooped up the delicate feline into her arms. It lay there contentedly and purred loudly, peering over at Megan curiously.

"Sapphire gets up and down by a tree that's just outside. If she knew Blaise was here, she'd have a fit. Sapphire hates him!" Helena giggled and dropped the cat onto her bed.

"So…" Helena prompted impatiently, "What do you think of my room?"

The Charm Tree

"Oh, it's great; I love it," Megan lied. In truth, she thought the room looked like a giant purple cake with white and silver icing.

"Yes, it's certainly better than that haunted house that Jared sleeps in."

"Haunted house—?" Megan spluttered, but she didn't get a chance to finish her sentence before Helena had grabbed her arm, dragged her over to a vanity, and plopped her down onto a violet-cushioned stool. Helena sat down beside Megan and began pulling costume jewelry out from an ornate box, trying on different pairs of dangly earrings and bracelets.

Megan began rummaging absent-mindedly through the contents of the box, and she couldn't help but compare herself to Helena as she peered at their reflections in the vanity mirror. Megan had inherited her mother's green eyes and auburn hair, which was pulled back into an untidy ponytail at the moment. She suddenly noticed with despair that her baggy, red sweatshirt seemed to be sporting a gravy stain from dinner.

As Megan watched Helena, she began to think of the prissy girls from her old school and of how they used to taunt her. The dark, empty feeling crept back into the pit of Megan's stomach as her thoughts returned to her new school, which she would be starting in the morning.

Presently, Megan noticed a picture of a man and a woman on the vanity table. The man was tall and blonde, while the woman had a dark complexion and brown, shoulder-length hair. The man had his arm around her, and they seemed very happy as they smiled at each other.

"Who are they?" asked Megan.

"Those are my parents," answered Helena. "Father grew up in this house and worked at the theatre. My mother came from the First Nations people, and she lived in the nearby mountains with her father. She loved the theatre and came to all of the big shows; that's how my parents met. They died in a car crash when Jared and I were three," Helena explained as she put down the rhinestone-studded tiara that she had been holding and tried to wipe away a tear secretly.

"I'm really sorry," said Megan as she felt a pang of guilt over her own minor troubles. "And to think that my biggest concern is what school will be like tomorrow."

Sapphire jumped up onto the vanity, and Helena began to stroke her silky fur. "You've got nothing to worry about," she said warmly. "Most of the kids at school are goofs, and no one has any fashion sense, but you'll be with me, and I don't take any garbage from them." Helena smiled and held up a pair of green earrings to Megan's ears. "I think these would go well with your eyes."

The Charm Tree

Megan smiled back and also began to pet Sapphire. The cat stretched out lazily and purred loudly, scattering half of the jewellery onto the floor. Maybe Helena wasn't so bad after all, Megan thought. She may act like a snob a little, but for once, Megan wouldn't be running away from her—she would be walking in with her.

★ 4 ★
The First Day

The next morning saw a mad rush as everybody in the Whittlebee household tried to get ready to go off to school or work. Six people sharing one bathroom was a nightmare. Megan munched on a piece of toast and peanut butter, while she rummaged through her suitcase, looking for a nice skirt and blouse.

"It's hopeless," she muttered to herself and reached for her favourite pair of jeans and a blue sweater. Having tried to do something decent with her hair, and having failed miserably, Megan quickly brushed it back into a ponytail.

"Just be yourself, honey. They'll love you; you'll see," her mother said as she handed Megan her jacket and backpack.

Presently, the doorbell rang, and Aunt Dolly ran to get it. It was Jared and Helena.

"Children, it's wonderful to see you!" Aunt Dolly gushed. "Won't you come in and have some breakfast with us?"

"Thank you, Mrs. Whittlebee," replied Jared, "but we really should be getting to school."

"Hurry up, Megan!" Blaise called as he rushed past his mother with his skateboard in one hand and a piece of chocolate cake in the other. Megan quickly wished her father good luck on his first day at the Mavilyn Theatre, kissed her mother and Nicholas—who tried to give her his bunny in a gesture of support—and dashed out the door.

Megan was happy to be walking to school with Blaise and the Mavilyns. She had only just arrived in Shansymoon, but already she was beginning to feel a slight sense of belonging. Megan was even more delighted when Jared handed her the book she had been looking at the evening before: *The Universe and the Beings Who Live There*.

"I thought you might like to borrow it," he said awkwardly before quickly catching up to Blaise.

Megan smiled as she put the book in her backpack.

As they walked, and Blaise attempted to use his skateboard on the icy sidewalks, the children discussed

The Charm Tree

the newest movies, video games and the strange people who passed them on the sidewalk. One man was wearing a black cape and raised his top hat to the children, and a woman in Gypsy garb stood on a corner playing a very old violin. Megan thought her music was enchanting, and she took two loonies out of her pocket and dropped them into the woman's open violin case. The woman smiled warmly and gave Megan a card with strange pictures and symbols on it. Megan didn't understand the symbols, but in the centre of the card was an image of a glowing, white bird, which was emerging from a dark pool of water with its wings outspread as if to take flight.

Megan was quite taken with the picture, but her concentration was interrupted as Blaise wondered aloud if the Math teacher, Mr. Brooks, would believe that his turtle ate his homework. Megan wouldn't have believed it either if she hadn't seen it with her own eyes.

"I used that excuse last week, and now that it's really happened, he won't believe me," moaned Blaise.

Helena adjusted her leather gloves. "Gertie Pertrude eats everything, Blaise. "I just know she ate my amber ring," she complained.

"It's not her fault," Blaise responded defensively, "she probably thought it was a caramel; Gertie loves caramels…," he added distractedly, as his attention had wandered to a plane that was flying overhead.

Jared and Megan burst out laughing, but as the children turned a corner, and Shansymoon Middle School came into view, a few of the butterflies fluttered back into Megan's stomach. Questions started racing through her mind: What would her new school be like? Would the other students like her? Would she be able to catch up on the work she had missed?

Once inside, Blaise and Jared went to their lockers and then on to homeroom, while Helena showed Megan to the Reception Office. Megan's parents had already completed her registration, so she just needed to receive her timetable and locker assignment. She was delighted to discover that she was to take most of her classes with her new friends.

Megan and Helena reached the homeroom after the last bell had rung; everyone was seated, and the teacher had begun the lesson. The whole class turned to stare at Megan and Helena as they walked in. Megan felt her face go red, and her eyes turned to the floor instinctively. Helena, however, remained undaunted.

"Ms. Crewitt, this is Megan Whittlebee. She just moved here from Ontario, and she will sit at the back of the room with me," Helena declared rather matter-of-factly.

Ms. Crewitt barely had a chance to respond before Helena took Megan's arm and began to escort her regally

The Charm Tree

to the back of the room. The class seemed to be astir with whispers as Megan took a seat behind Blaise, and Helena sat down behind Jared.

"Oh—well—welcome, Megan, welcome," spluttered Ms. Crewitt, who seemed to be a little taken aback by Helena's late, and somewhat abrupt, entrance, but she made no attempt to reprimand her. "We were just discussing—uh—chapter seven in our English Readers. You can—you can share with Helena for now."

Megan had to hide a smile behind her notebook; Helena could even intimidate the teacher! Megan looked over at Helena, and she couldn't help but wish that she had just a smidgeon of her boldness.

As the class resumed, and the other students returned their attention to Ms. Crewitt (or the various activities they had been engaged in when Megan and Helena had entered), Megan took a moment to look around the room. Various pictures of famous English writers hung on the walls, and some advertisements of upcoming plays were posted on a message board.

Megan saw a poster for Shakespeare's *A Midsummer Night's Dream*, which depicted a funny-looking man with the head of a donkey. Fairies were flittering all around him, and standing on a tree stump next to the man, was a particularly beautiful fairy with golden hair and glittering wings. Megan was suddenly reminded of her father's story of the fairy he had seen, and she pulled the silver chain with the crystal trinket out of her sweater. It shone in the morning light, which was pouring into the classroom. Megan's father had claimed to see the fairy in the very mountains Megan could see through the classroom windows.

"But fairies aren't real, *are* they?" Megan muttered to herself under her breath. She reached into her bag and pulled out *The Universe and the Beings Who Live There*. Megan hid the book behind her notebook, while she flipped through its pages. The text looked complicated, but the pictures were very interesting. Megan saw drawings of ghosts, angels and odd-looking aliens. Megan flipped over another page and gasped. There, to her astonishment, was a picture of a tiny person with wings! As far as Megan knew, fairies only existed in fairy tales. Megan read some of the text beneath the picture eagerly:

> "Fairies—along with pixies, elves, gnomes and other beings that are often relegated to the worlds of fiction and fantasy—reside in a realm lower than our Earth plane. Though they generally remain within their own world, fairies may choose to cross the veil separating the worlds, which are connected by a magnificent …"

The Charm Tree

Megan's concentration was harshly interrupted when something swooped by her face, nearly hitting her.

"Sorry," Jared whispered. "I was trying to pass a note to Blaise."

Megan gave the note to Blaise, then she slipped the book back into her bag. She pulled out a pen and started taking notes. If fairies *were* real, she thought, they likely weren't going to help her catch up on two months of missed English work.

———⋙◆⋘———

The rest of the morning classes progressed without much incident. Megan sat with her new friends, and she only had to endure curious glances from the other students. During the breaks, Megan was delighted to finally have people to hang out with. She was amazed by all of the things Blaise could do with a skateboard. Helena provided good competition for the crowd's attention, however, by displaying some impressive ballet moves.

After lunch, the children had Math class, and fortunately for Blaise, Mr. Brooks *did* believe his turtle incident.

"He says it's happened to him six times!" Blaise said ecstatically as he plopped down into his seat next to the window. "What a great day this is turning out to be!"

Megan had to agree; so far everything seemed to be going much better than she had hoped. There were no jokes and sneers nor any nasty notes that found their way onto her desk, and there was no chocolate pudding on her seat at lunch!

Later on in the day, as the others headed off to the gymnasium, Megan made her way to her Music class. Unfortunately, the Gym class was already full, but Megan didn't mind this so much, since she felt she wasn't very good at sports anyway. Megan felt her luck must surely be changing, and this gave her a little boost of confidence.

Megan was looking up at the number on the door as she entered the classroom, and she accidentally walked right into a girl with long, red hair. As the girl whipped around, Megan found herself face-to-face with the girl she had bumped into at the airport, and her newfound confidence suddenly sank down through the green and black-tiled floor. The girl sneered at Megan.

"Why don't you watch where you're going!" she spat furiously. However, when the girl had taken a good look at Megan, her demeanor suddenly changed, and a slow, malicious grin began to spread across her face. Megan's spirits plummeted. Unfortunately, the girl seemed to remember her as well.

"So, *you're* the new girl," the redheaded girl said silkily with an evil glint in her eyes. "There must be something

The Charm Tree

horribly wrong with your legs, since you just can't seem to walk without running people down. But don't worry, I'm sure we'll be able to take care of that problem for you," she added as her eyes narrowed to dangerous slits. Megan was sure she could see orange fire shooting out from those slits.

A girl with brown, curly hair approached and stood beside her. "She's friends with Helena Mavilyn, Lacy," the girl said.

"Really?" the redheaded girl replied, obviously undaunted. "Well, Helena's not here, is she?"

Just when Megan was beginning to think that things were looking very dire for her indeed, the teacher bustled into the room and set his leather briefcase on his desk.

"Lacy, Georgina, can you take your seats please?"

"Yes, Mr. Lawder," they both replied with mock sweetness. The seats were arranged in two semicircular rows that faced the blackboard, and the two girls sat down in the second row.

Mr. Lawder walked over to Megan and introduced himself, and he told her she could take a seat anywhere she liked. Megan quickly went to the other side of the room and sat at the end of the first row—as far from the girls as she could get.

Mr. Lawder began the Music lesson, and Megan noticed that every time he turned to write something on the blackboard, little pieces of rolled-up paper landed in her hair or on her notebook. As she glanced behind, Lacy and Georgina waved and giggled. Megan sighed and slouched down in her seat; this was a scene she knew all too well.

Megan counted the minutes until the class ended, and when the 3:30 bell finally rang, she grabbed her things and quickly made for the door. Mr. Lawder, however, called her back and offered Megan the choice of playing the flute or the clarinet (the only instruments that were left). Megan hastily grabbed the clarinet case and sheet music that Mr. Lawder handed her, and she turned for the door. Suddenly, she breathed a sigh of relief—Lacy and Georgina had gone, but standing outside in the hall, waiting for her, was Helena, with Blaise and Jared standing behind her.

"Am I ever glad to see you guys," Megan said as the children made their way to their lockers to get their things. Once outside and on their way home, Megan told the others about her encounter with Lacy.

"Lacy Reilly's in the seventh grade, and she's a fox!" replied Blaise enthusiastically.

Helena shot him an icy look that persuaded him to add, "I mean—she has the slyness of a fox; you'd better steer clear of her, Meg."

The Charm Tree

"Lacy tried to intimidate Helena once, but good ol' sis sent her running to the girls' washroom with tears gushing down her face, didn't you Helena?" added Jared.

"That's right!" Helena replied. "Underneath all that lank, red hair is a scared little mouse. You just have to show her that you're not going to take anything she dishes out, Megan."

Megan thought that was less easy then it sounded. Once the children reached Snicker Doodle Street, Helena and Jared invited Megan and Blaise to come over to their house. After Megan had called home for permission (Blaise didn't feel the need to bother), they all headed to the Carnival Room. On the way, the children passed by a large, shiny suit of armour, which was standing next to the banister of the blue staircase. Megan didn't remember seeing it there before.

"Hi Uncle Francis," Jared said offhandedly as the children passed. No sound or movement came from the armour. Once in the doorway of the Carnival Room, Blaise took a penny from his pocket and flicked it at the suit of armour. It ricocheted off the metal helmet, causing a loud bang to reverberate within. The suit or armour turned and shook its fist at the children as they passed through the purple hangings.

Megan was delighted that Helena and Jared had chosen this particular room. What she needed was cheering up, and if the Carnival Room couldn't succeed, nothing could. Helena and Jared fell onto the pink couch, which was adorned with big, fluffy pillows, while Blaise hopped up onto one of the carousel ponies. He made different ludicrous faces each time his pony came around. Megan chose a round, bright yellow pouf to sit on, but she screamed out immediately as a panel opened up, and she fell right through it.

"Sorry about that," Jared said as he helped Megan up. "That's the trick chair." Jared gestured to a purple, velvet armchair, and Megan sat down gingerly.

Out from behind a life-size, teetering jack-in-the-box crept a silky, black cat. Apparently, Sapphire had been enjoying a comfortable snooze before the children had arrived and awoken her. After stretching sleepy muscles, Sapphire let out an elegant "meow" as a greeting before proceeding to clean her already pristine coat.

Presently, Baxter entered the room carrying a tray with liquorice and pop, and he hesitated as he surveyed the flamboyant room disapprovingly. He was about to place the tray onto the yellow pouf when he remembered the trick panel, and with an impatient sniff, the butler chose a small, red table instead. Blaise hopped down from the carousel, and the children started in on the contents of the tray immediately.

The Charm Tree

"This is the life, I tell ya," exclaimed Blaise as he drank his lime-coloured pop through a liquorice stick.

Megan had to agree. She would give anything to live in a house like this, and she said so.

"Helena and I go exploring sometimes," Jared replied, "but even we haven't discovered all of the house's secrets yet."

"Wait until you see the theatre!" added Helena excitedly. "So many staircases and creepy corridors. I take my ballet lessons there, and I even have my own dressing room!"

Jared suggested they all stop by there the following day after school, and Megan agreed that it would be a good idea. She wanted to see where her father would be working, and Megan had to admit that her interest had been piqued.

"All right," Blaise replied. "Just so long as I don't have to watch *twinkle toes* prance across the stage in a fluffy tutu." A pillow flew across the room and hit Blaise in the face. Instantly, a full-blown battle ensued amongst all of the children, which sent up a cloud of feathers and foam. Sapphire retreated quickly into the safety of her cozy hideaway behind the jack-in-the-box.

In the midst of all the shouting and laughter, Mrs. Mavilyn swept into the room in a flowing, blue gown, followed by Baxter, and she announced that Megan and Blaise were wanted at home for dinner.

"I begged them to let you stay, since we're having lobster and candy apples tonight—only red foods on Mondays you know—but your parents are very interested in learning how your first day at school went, Megan," explained Mrs. Mavilyn.

"Yes, it is a pity that you both can't stay," added Baxter dryly as he surveyed the room, which looked as though a feather storm had passed through it.

Megan and Blaise said their goodbyes and grabbed their things. As they walked home, leaving a trail of feathers in the snow behind them, Megan came to the conclusion that her first day in Shansymoon Creek had been a decidedly interesting one.

★ 5 ★
Mayhem at Mavilyn Theatre

The next morning found another whirlwind of commotion as the Whittlebees got ready to face another day. Even though Megan had set her alarm clock fifteen minutes earlier in the hopes of getting some prime shower time, somehow the bathroom was occupied every time she checked. When Megan finally found the room empty, she had to cut through a dense fog of steam and nearly tripped over half a dozen wet towels spread across the floor.

Aunt Dolly had dropped a box of her doodads on the foyer floor, and she was beside herself trying to collect them all, while Uncle George submerged his green-checkered tie accidentally while attempting to feed the fish.

"Is that orange one supposed to be floating upside down like that, Dad?" asked Blaise.

Nicholas was having fun attempting to cover up the hideous gold and green wallpaper in the dining room with his breakfast, while his father slurped down some form of soggy cereal in brown milk.

"Have a nice day at work, sweetie," Laura Whittlebee said as she kissed her husband on the cheek.

Tom Whittlebee used his briefcase to shield himself from some flying mush as he ran for the door. "Don't forget to stop by after school today, Megan," he yelled. "I want to show you some of our sets and props for the upcoming shows."

A moment later the doorbell rang, and Megan almost broke her neck on some large beads and buttons as she came skidding across the foyer floor to answer it.

"Whew!" exclaimed Jared, who had poked his head through the open door. "This is a madhouse. And I thought *our* house was strange."

"I know, I love it!" declared Blaise happily as he munched on some cold pizza for breakfast. "I just don't know if Mrs. Thompson is going to believe that Sapphire peed all over my history assignment."

"It's your fault for calling her a mangy fur ball," replied Helena, who was looking as cool and impeccable as usual in her white slacks and purple coat.

The Charm Tree

"Well, you have to admit, her hairstyle is pretty outrageous. I think Mrs. Thompson is stuck in the eighties." Blaise laughed loudly at his own joke.

"*Ha ha*," Helena answered, "you should talk—your parents are flashbacks from the seventies!"

Blaise knew when he had been beat, so he contented himself with stuffing his face in silence. As the children walked, Megan observed the imposing theatre across the way. Even though she wasn't looking forward to another day at Shansymoon Middle School, she felt a tinge of excitement at the prospect of visiting the old, Gothic-looking building. She tried to imagine her father as a boy, running through the halls and tumbling through secret trapdoors. Megan giggled to herself; it was something she could envision quite easily.

Megan's second day at her new school was filled with breakneck flights from class to class and several around-the-corner glances to see if the redheaded monster was in the vicinity. Megan breathed a sigh of relief knowing that she didn't share any classes with Lacy Reilly that day, but she still didn't want to run into her in the halls.

"Relax, Meg," said Blaise as the children made their way towards the cafeteria at lunchtime. "If Lacy gives you any trouble, just give her a fistful of badness," he said as he punched the air.

"Speak of the devil," whispered Jared, nudging Blaise in the ribs, as Lacy had just walked out of a classroom directly in front of them, followed closely by Georgina.

"Uh—hi, Lacy," Blaise muttered lamely as he fidgeted with his shirt. "Ah—I sure hope they don't serve that mystery meat chili for lunch again today." He let out a forced laugh as Lacy sniffed haughtily and walked ahead and into the cafeteria.

Jared nearly choked on his bubblegum as he burst out laughing. "Yeah, a fistful of badness all right!" he cried sarcastically.

"Shut up," answered Blaise as his face quickly turned the colour of Lacy's hair.

"Oh, Blaise, just don't say anything to her," Megan cried as the children walked into the lunchroom. "I don't want any more attention drawn to me."

"Why ever not?" asked Helena, who plunked herself down at a table at the front of the room, closest to the door and the cafeteria line-up, where everyone could see her. "Grandmother says that a little exposure never hurts one's career."

Megan looked at Helena incredulously, while Blaise twirled his finger at his temple again.

When the children were finished eating their lunches, Blaise and Jared moved over to a table of boys and joined an animated discussion about the newest martial arts

The Charm Tree

video game. As Helena excused herself to "powder her nose," Megan pulled out her schedule to find out what class they had next. As she did so, Megan felt a presence lurking over her shoulder, and the hairs on the back of her neck began to rise. Megan turned her head to see, none other than, Lacy Reilly leering down at her with a sinister grin. Georgina stood nearby, attempting to keep a straight face. Megan felt her own face flush.

"Hey, Megan," said Lacy. "What's up?"

"Not much," Megan managed to answer, though she knew her voice sounded weak.

"All finished your lunch I see," said Lacy as she sat down next to Megan. "Why don't you let me take that empty tray over to the counter for you?" she asked in a sickly-sweet voice.

"Thanks," Megan responded uncertainly, feeling that Lacy must have gone stark raving mad.

"But look, you haven't finished your milk yet. Here, why don't you just take this back—" Lacy dropped the half-filled carton into Megan's lap, splashing milk onto her sweater and soiling her jeans.

"Oh, I'm *so* sorry," Lacy declared derisively. "It must be *absolutely* horrifying to have a drink spilled all over you, and right in front of everyone too!"

As Lacy and Georgina walked away, laughing, Megan noticed the people in the lunch line-up staring at her. She turned away quickly and began rummaging through her bag for something to soak up the milk with. When she found nothing, Megan got up and ran for the washroom with her bag held in front of her, nearly knocking down Helena on the way.

"What's wrong?" asked Helena as she followed Megan back into the washroom. Through frustrated and humiliated sobs, Megan explained what had happened as she dabbed at her clothes with paper towel. This was something she remembered all too well.

"That mean witch!" exclaimed Helena. "We'll get Lacy back for this, don't you worry!"

"No," replied Megan, "That will only make it worse. Maybe Lacy will leave me alone now that we're even."

"You're mad!" cried Helena. "You can't let someone do that to you. You've got to stand up for yourself, Megan."

As the bell rang for the next class, Megan took off her outer sweater and tried to tie it around her waist so that the wet mark on her jeans wouldn't show.

During her afternoon classes, Megan found it difficult to concentrate, and she contented herself with doodling in her notebook, while Jared eagerly took notes, Helena played with her pink, furry pen and Blaise stared at the ceiling absent-mindedly with his jaw hanging open.

Megan let out an audible sigh as a deep gloom settled down upon her. As far as she could tell, Shansymoon

The Charm Tree

was just another Shadyville. Sure, it was slightly more bizarre and colourful, and the town had more than its share of oddballs, but at its heart it was just the same. Misery seemed to follow Megan wherever she went; she just couldn't escape it, and this thought filled her with a terrible dread.

As the children left school later that afternoon, Helena, Blaise and Jared each discussed what they would have done if they had been in Megan's place:

"I would have grabbed some cream corn and rubbed it in Lacy's face before starting the food fight of the century!" exclaimed Blaise with enthusiasm.

"I would have drawn a caricature of Lacy with snakes coming out of her head and spewing milk everywhere," added Jared. "And I would have made a hundred copies and pasted them all over the school!"

Blaise laughed loudly and hit Jared's shoulder. "Snakes! Perfect Jared!…What's a carrot-chur…?"

"Are you *kidding* me!" exclaimed Helena. "If that witch had poured milk all over me, I would have dragged her outside by her hair and thrown her into a dirty snow bank."

Both Blaise and Jared looked over at Helena with awe and more than a little uneasiness. They knew she wasn't exaggerating. Blaise moved a few steps away just to be on the safe side.

"Well, that's easy for you guys to say now," said Megan, "but you didn't have it happen to you in front of the whole school. Everyone was looking at me, and I just wanted to become invisible."

"Once you're inside Mavilyn Theatre, you won't think about Lacy Reilly anymore," Jared said encouragingly. "There are way too many cool things to see and do."

"Yeah, like my dressing room!" added Helena with delight.

By this time, the children had reached the fence surrounding the theatre grounds. Megan liked the tall, iron bars and the many hedges and bushes she could see within. As they walked in through the gate and started toward the theatre, Megan saw many paths leading off in different directions, and she noticed that some paths seemed to lead into enclosures created by the hedges and trees. Inside these enclosures, Megan saw fountains, stone benches and some statues.

As the children rounded a bend in the path, Megan thought she perceived movement out of the corner of her eye within one of the hedged-in areas. However, when she looked again, Megan saw only a stone statue of a beautiful mermaid that was perched on top of a rock with a pouty look on her face. Further along, there stood two

The Charm Tree

statues of short, elflike creatures with slanted eyes and huge, mischievous grins. They had their arms around each other's shoulders and appeared to be in a state of merriment. As Megan stared at the statues, her breath caught in her chest. Had one of them winked at her just now?

Blaise followed Megan's gaze and ran over to the statues. "Aren't they awesome?" he asked. "Last summer I put mud in their noses every day—I wanted them to have perma-bougers." Blaise picked up a twig and put it in the open mouth of one of the statues. "There, now he's smoking."

Blaise ran off to catch up with the others. After a moment, Megan turned to follow; she had a queer feeling in her stomach. *Must have been a trick of the flickering light shining through the tree branches*, Megan thought to herself.

As she approached Mavilyn Theatre, Megan couldn't help but feel awed by its size and grandness. Stone dragons peered down from deep alcoves above the oak doors, which were carved in strange, intricate designs. The golden light pouring out from thin, arched windows seemed inviting despite the imposing appearance of the dark building.

Jared pulled open the heavy doors, and the children entered into a bright foyer with a cream-coloured marble floor and ornately sculpted walls. From here, the children ascended a large staircase and entered the lobby. There were several people bustling about; some were dressed in fancy costumes, while others were rushing around with props.

Presently, Mrs. Mavilyn and Megan's father entered into the lobby from a large doorway that appeared to lead into the auditorium. Tom Whittlebee looked flustered, but Mrs. Mavilyn was positively glowing.

"Children!" she called. "How simply marvelous to see you, and how fortunate—you've arrived just in time to witness our mayhem."

"Oh—yes," spluttered Megan's father. "Something has gone terribly wrong! Hundreds of costumes have been hidden beneath the seats in the auditorium, and entire sets have gone missing!"

"Perhaps something *has* gone terribly wrong, or maybe something has gone wonderfully right!" added Mrs. Mavilyn with a cheery smile. "I've never liked that particular production, and perhaps this is a sign. Now we can choose something far more interesting to present next week."

"But we haven't the time to prepare, Mrs. Mavilyn!" cried Tom Whittlebee, before he went rushing after a stagehand, who seemed to be carrying a broken lamppost prop.

The Charm Tree

"Your father seems to have forgotten how things are done in Mavilyn Theatre," Mrs. Mavilyn whispered to Megan. "He'll quickly rediscover it I think," she added with a wink.

"Go on, children," she added to the others. "I think you should find something to amuse yourselves with in the back."

As Mrs. Mavilyn sauntered off, humming to herself serenely amidst the chaos, Jared called the others to follow him. "This way is the fastest," he explained and entered into the auditorium. The others followed Jared into a vast room filled with plush, blue seats that lead down to a large stage.

The children walked past many disgruntled actors and stage help, who were looking under seats and pulling out all manner of strange things. One man pulled out what looked like a wand, and he started yelping immediately as the wand shot out bursts of purple and silver glitter. A woman pulled out a white dove, which puffed up its feathers in agitation. With an angry flutter of its wings, the dove took off to settle onto the railing of one of the upper balconies.

The children climbed onto the stage and turned to the right, pushing past a sea of midnight blue, velvet hangings. The backstage was even more chaotic than the rest of the building. People were bustling about everywhere amongst sets and scaffolding and tables piled high with costumes and props. Some people were shouting angry curses, and one man could do nothing but stand still and laugh hysterically.

"You've gotta *love* this place!" exclaimed Blaise with glee as the children passed through into a more secluded and quiet area of the scene dock.

Megan looked around with interest at all of the props. There were dangling, golden stars; old, knotty oaks and gigantic mushrooms. "This place *is* great," she said. "We could put on a play for ourselves with all of this stuff."

"Yes, let's do that!" chimed in Helena. "Come on, let's go into the costume room and pick out something to wear. Helena led the others into a large room with aisle after aisle of hanging costumes.

Soon enough the children had chosen their outfits. Helena had draped herself in a sparkling, pink princess's gown, while Blaise sported pirate gear, complete with cutlass and wooden leg. Megan had chosen a purple wizard's cloak and hat, while Jared had pulled on a hairy werewolf costume.

Helena proceeded to dictate the storyline of the play; however, the loud voices of Jared and Blaise soon drowned her out.

"Argh! Get off, I say. That mushroom be mine!" yelled Blaise with his drawn sword.

The Charm Tree

Jared howled at the silvery moon hanging above before threatening to chew off Blaise's other leg. Megan muttered curses at the werewolf, and she started poking at it with her golden wand, while Helena waved her glittering scepter about wildly, attempting to create order.

Suddenly, one of the huge, pointed stars fell down from the ceiling onto a spotted fawn, causing it to fall over unceremoniously. The children froze.

Before anyone could speak, a bird's nest was snatched off of a branch of one of the gnarled, English oaks, before a hooded figure was spied disappearing behind a statue of a sphinx—giggling!

"What the—?" muttered Blaise.

"It's just Uncle Francis playing tricks again," said Helena, although even she didn't seem thoroughly convinced. Suddenly, a head appeared between two white pillars causing the children to scream and jump.

"Let's go home, kids," Tom Whittlebee said in an exhausted voice. "Dinner should be ready soon, and there's not much more that I can do here tonight."

The children took off their costumes and collected their things. As they followed Megan's father back through the grounds in the growing twilight, Megan reflected on the oddness of Shansymoon. A cold, clean breeze blew over her face, and Megan breathed it in gratefully. Her contemplation was interrupted, however, by the mumbling of Blaise and Jared behind her.

"He was much too short to have been Uncle Francis," Jared whispered.

"I think the faun ate my Math textbook," Blaise whispered back.

As they were nearing the iron gate, Megan glanced over at the sultry mermaid. She was still adorning her rock and staring out sadly at invisible ships passing by. Megan's gaze moved farther down, and her breath suddenly caught in her chest. Where there had been a pair of ludicrous-looking elfish creatures just earlier that afternoon, there was now only an empty stone platform.

"But where—?" she uttered aloud.

"What is it, Doodle Bug?" her father asked.

"Oh—nothing," Megan answered, shaking her head in bewilderment. "I must have been mistaken." But deep inside, Megan began to feel something stirring, and high above, the real stars twinkled.

★ 6 ★
A Wish is Heard

The next weeks were busy for everyone. Jared helped Megan catch up to the other students with her schoolwork, and Helena insisted on walking with Megan from class to class in case Lacy showed up. Megan's father was already happily entrenched within his new job and working hard on the forthcoming Christmas productions, while Megan's mother kept herself busy looking after Nicholas and searching for a house (an activity she happily fell back on when she needed to escape Aunt Dolly's incessant invitations to make Christmas crafts). Uncle George was preparing final examinations and drowning in essays to be marked ("If I have to deal with one more student requesting an extension…!").

One day, as Megan was lounging on the back of a sea serpent prop at Mavilyn Theatre, playing squeaky notes absent-mindedly on her clarinet, it dawned on her that she had already lived in Shansymoon Creek for over a month. The whole town was now covered with a thick blanket of glittering snow, and Christmas lights shone out from every tree and window.

It was amazing to Megan how quickly she had become accustomed to this strange, new town and people. Things were not going too badly either; holidays were fast approaching, and besides the occasional nasty note or snide comment in the hallways, Megan had not had to endure many more incidents with Lacy Reilly. Nicholas was crawling now, and he often contented himself with sitting on Aunt Dolly's doodads or poking at Gertie Pertrude with his green bunny, which was now beginning to look more like a grey and tattered lump with a couple of whiskers sticking out here and there.

As Megan stared up at the wooden rafters of the scene dock ceiling, she let her thoughts drift to the stone statues of the elves out in the grounds. Since her first day visiting Mavilyn Theatre, Megan had trudged out into the snow to inspect them several times, but they were always there, standing on their stone base and smiling up at her with those same silly grins. Blaise had built miniature snowmen

The Charm Tree

on top of their heads, which only added to their ludicrous appearance.

Megan hadn't mentioned her experience to anyone else because she didn't want them to think she was crazy. After all, stone statues don't just get up and walk around. Now she was beginning to wonder if she had only imagined it all. It had just been her father's stories and the book that Jared had loaned her that were getting to her, Megan thought. Megan was drawn out of her reverie mercilessly by the sound of a book snapping shut.

"Aha!" cried Blaise. "Got you, slimy beetle! I knew this English Reader would come in handy someday."

"Why do you always have to be so disgusting?" cried Helena, who had been styling the long, green tresses of a mermaid prop.

"Hey, you should be thanking me," responded Blaise with an unconvincing wounded tone. "That's one less creepy crawly that will find its way into your ballet slippers."

"That might be rather helpful, Blaise, if I *had* ballet slippers," Helena exclaimed. "My last pair went missing three days ago. Would you happen to know anything about that?" she asked, eyeing Blaise suspiciously.

"How would I know?" Blaise responded, suddenly getting irritated. "Why don't you ask that freaky feline of yours? She's always stealing things."

Jared, who had been leaning against a ship anchor, lost in his Geography assignment, let out a chuckle. His laugh was immediately answered by a giggle from the ceiling.

"Whoa!" Jared uttered. "Is there an echo in here?"

"Hey, what's that?" asked Megan as she spotted something fluttering down from the rafters. It lodged itself in the branches of a leafless, spooky-looking tree.

"It's my dreamcatcher," cried Helena as she moved closer for a better look. "But it was in my dressing room; how did it get here?"

Blaise climbed up onto one of the giant mushrooms and snatched the object down from the tree. It was a large ring with webbing in the middle that was decorated with feathers and beads.

"What is it?" asked Megan.

"It was a gift from our Grandfather White Bear," explained Jared as he too got up to look at it. "It originated in the Ojibwa culture. If you hang the dreamcatcher above your bed, it will trap the bad dreams inside it and let only the good dreams pass through."

Megan looked at the object with interest. She often had very vivid dreams at night, and many of them were rather unpleasant.

"Grandfather lives in the nearby mountains in a log house," explained Helena. "Jared and I are going to visit

The Charm Tree

him next week before Christmas. Hey, Megan, why don't you come with us?"

"Yeah, Megan, it'll be fun," added Jared. "There's tons of snow up there, and we can go sledding and skating."

Blaise jumped down from the mushroom with an indignant look on his face. "Hey, I want to go to Grandpa's too!"

Megan looked at him in surprise.

"What?" Blaise asked with a bemused look. "He said I can call him that."

Megan laughed before agreeing to ask her parents for permission to go. As the boys began to plan their holiday activities excitedly, and Helena returned to the tresses of her mermaid, Megan began to sense a darkness overshadowing the children's revelry. It was oppressive and seemed to weigh heavily in Megan's chest. She sensed danger.

Within moments, Mrs. Mavilyn came rushing into the room. She was wearing a long, luxurious-looking, black coat that appeared in stark contrast to her white face. "Children, we've got to go to the hospital. Now, I'm afraid!" she exclaimed. "Nicholas is very sick. Come quickly!"

Megan's heart flew up into her throat. For a moment the other children looked at Megan awkwardly, not knowing what to do or say.

"Come on now!" prompted Mrs. Mavilyn. "Baxter is waiting outside with the car."

Megan and the others quickly grabbed their things and ran towards the main entrance of the theatre. *Not again*, Megan thought to herself as she felt a painful wave shoot through her chest. *Why does my brother have to be sick? Why can't it be someone else's brother?*

Everyone was silent during the ride to the hospital. For once, Blaise was not taunting Baxter, and Helena was not hurling projectiles at Blaise's head. Megan stared out the car window at the snow that was falling gently under the golden light from the street lamps. Outside, everything seemed calm and serene, but inside, Megan felt like everything was crashing down.

Once in the hospital, Mrs. Mavilyn led the children to the waiting room. When Megan had spotted her parents, she ran to them and fell into their arms.

Megan's mother was crying, but her father tried to be reassuring.

"Don't worry yourself, Lollipop, everything is going to be fine."

Megan wanted to believe her father—she really did. She and the others sat down. No one had much to say. Megan didn't like the feel of the place at all. She didn't like the sounds or the smells or the people in their white and green uniforms. As Megan watched the nurses and

The Charm Tree

doctors walk by, she wondered where they were going and what they were going to do. She wondered if they were going to help Nicky.

For Megan, everything started to move in slow motion as a sensation of overwhelming helplessness swept over her. She wanted to grab her brother and run home. Surely Nicky would get better if he were in his own crib with his green bunny. He would get better if he were with his family and friends, not with strangers who didn't know him or what he likes.

Sometime later—Megan couldn't tell how long—a nurse entered the waiting room and told Megan's parents that they could see Nicholas now. Megan's father suggested that Megan go home with the Mavilyns and Blaise.

"But I want to stay here with Nicky!" Megan pleaded as she grasped her mother's arm tightly.

"I know, Megan," her mother said, "but it's probably best that you don't see him tonight. It's better for you to go home and get some rest. You'll get to see Nicky soon, and you've got school tomorrow."

Megan was outraged. How could her mother expect her to go to school when her little brother was in the hospital? Megan started to protest, but Mrs. Mavilyn cut her off.

"Your mother is right, dear," she said. "Nicholas is in the best possible hands right now. Why don't you come home with us and spend the night with Helena?"

"Yes, come home with us," chimed in Helena. "You can sleep in my room."

As everyone watched her, Megan felt a lump rise in her throat, and she felt hot tears coming to her eyes. She wanted them all to stop looking at her. Megan agreed to go reluctantly, and she gave her parents a last hug before leaving with the Mavilyns.

Baxter stopped by her aunt and uncle's house so that Megan could pack an overnight bag. Blaise was also given permission to sleep over, so he quickly threw some things into a plastic garbage bag, and then they were off to Mavilyn Mansion. Once they had pulled into the driveway, Baxter opened the car door for Megan and grabbed her bag from the trunk. The light pouring out from the windows of the huge house gave Megan some comfort. Inside, it was warm, and burning candles emitted a soft glow.

Once in Helena's room, the girls found Sapphire curled up on the bed. The cat opened her eyes and let her tail unfurl when the girls approached. Megan placed her bag onto the bed and opened it. Tears of frustration welled up in her eyes once more—she had remembered

The Charm Tree

to bring her schoolbooks, a toothbrush and a change of clothes—everything, it seemed, except pajamas.

"Don't worry, Megan," Helena said as she grabbed an extra nightgown from her dresser. "You can borrow one of mine."

After Megan had changed into the warm, flannel gown, she sat down on the edge of the bed and started petting Sapphire. The cat stretched its long, sleek body before getting up and jumping off the bed.

"Where is she going?" asked Megan with a slight sniffle.

"Probably off to torment Blaise," answered Helena, who had changed into a pink, frilly nightgown and was combing through her long, dark hair. "Let's follow her."

Megan and Helena followed Sapphire to the top of the blue staircase and then down another darkened hallway. Halfway down the hall, Sapphire slid silkily into the pale light of a slightly ajar doorway. Helena paused to knock and was answered by Jared's voice telling her to come in.

Megan felt astonishment upon first sight of the cavernous room. The floor seemed to be made of some kind of stone tile, and the walls were papered with wine-red silk. Black, velvet hangings covered the high windows as well as a mahogany, four-poster bed. A fire roared in a large, Gothic-looking fireplace, and griffins peered down menacingly from the mantle. The flames flickered in the griffins' crimson, bejeweled eyes causing Megan to feel as though the creatures were leering down at her.

"This room is great," Megan commented, causing Helena to shoot her a look of utter disgust. "Thanks," Jared replied. He and Blaise were already in their pajamas and were sitting on an ornate carpet near the fire. The boys seemed to be fiddling with a miniature replica of an old, spooky-looking house.

"Ooooh, you're playing with your dollhouse," Helena said as she sat down eagerly on the carpet. Megan sat down too and began to inspect the house, which had been opened on hinges.

"This is *not* a dollhouse," Jared replied with indignation. "I'll have you know that the maid has fallen through the trapdoor in the pantry, and the mad scientist just got his arm caught in his own secret, sliding door."

"Mayhem descends as the mad scientist's experiment goes awry, and his cherished Doberman becomes a ghoulish creature that devours the entire household before escaping to chow down on the village folk!" Blaise added with relish.

"Here, Megan, you can be the ghost who lives in the attic," Jared said as he handed her a small figure of a pale woman all in white.

The Charm Tree

"She glows in the dark," Helena added enthusiastically.

Megan tried to smile and join in the fun, but her concern for Nicholas was all too apparent to her friends.

"Are you okay?" Jared asked.

"Yeah," Megan responded weakly. "Nicky's been taken to the hospital before, and he always comes home fine. I'm sure he'll be all right. I just wish there was something I could do to make him better," Megan said as a tear fell from her cheek.

Just then, the crystal trinket that was hanging from Megan's neck began to glow with a dull, pink light, and the other children stared.

"Hey, what's going on with your necklace?" Blaise asked.

"I don't know," Megan responded. "It must be catching the light from the fireplace."

Helena put her arm around Megan's shoulders. "If it makes you feel any better, Megan, we wish we could do something for Nicky too."

"Yeah," the two boys agreed in unison as they huddled around Megan as well.

The fire rose up momentarily, and sparks shot out of the fireplace causing the children to jump and Helena to shout out. Sapphire scampered out of her darkened corner (where she had been chewing on something that suspiciously resembled Blaise's Geography assignment) and bolted out of the room.

The children broke down into peels of laughter. It had been a long and stressful day, and they were all ready to turn in for the night.

As Megan lay in bed that night, she watched the dying embers in Helena's fireplace and said a silent prayer for her little brother. Tears came to her eyes as she remembered what her friends had said in front of Jared's fireplace. Megan knew their words had been heartfelt—if it came to it, they would do everything in their power to help Nicky.

Later that night, Megan dreamed of a tree. It's silvery, moonlit branches swayed gently in an icy wind…

★ 7 ★
Trip to the Mountains

Megan awoke with a start as she felt something land on her chest. Groggily, she blinked and peered up into a pair of luminous, yellow eyes that had a swishing, black tail somewhere behind them. Sapphire was purring loudly and padding her feet softly on Megan's chest.

Megan knew it was early. She glanced over at Helena, who was still asleep soundly with the covers pulled high over her head. Megan scooped up Sapphire and made her way quietly to the bedroom door. She peered out into the hallway and was confronted with utter silence and two long rows of closed doors that faded into the darkness. Megan had the queer sensation that even the house was sleeping.

With Sapphire still in her arms, Megan slipped out of Helena's room and made her way to the top of the blue staircase. She set down the black cat, who immediately turned down the hallway leading to the boys' room. Sapphire sat and watched the closed doorway eagerly with her tail swishing from side to side.

Up to no good, Megan thought to herself and smiled as she began to descend the large staircase. Once at the bottom, a delicious smell hit Megan's nose, and she spotted a warm glow spilling out from under a door at the end of the hallway, just past the dining room. Megan walked to the door and slowly pushed it open. Inside was a large, but cozy, kitchen with a fire roaring in a fireplace against the far wall, and Mrs. Mavilyn was standing at the stove in a long, crimson dressing gown. The older woman turned to Megan and greeted her with a warm smile.

"I suspected you might be up early," she said, "so I thought I would whip up some of my special pancakes. Take a seat, Megan; they'll be ready in jiffy."

Megan sat down at a wooden table in the centre of the room. She didn't feel like talking to anyone just at that moment, but she *was* famished. It suddenly occurred to her that they had all skipped dinner the evening before in their hasty trip to the hospital. And besides, Megan preferred the warm and bright kitchen to the rest of the house, which seemed cold and lonely just now.

The Charm Tree

"There you go—Sadie's Pancake Surprise," Mrs. Mavilyn said in a cheery voice as she placed a plate of very large pancakes smothered in butter and rich syrup in front of Megan. Megan smiled as she noticed what looked like Smarties poking out of her golden pancakes.

"Thank you," Megan said as she dove into her breakfast hungrily. She wanted desperately to ask Mrs. Mavilyn if she had any news about her brother, but she was frightened of what the answer might be. Instead, Megan chose to enjoy her time in the warm kitchen with Mrs. Mavilyn for as long as she could. Mrs. Mavilyn seemed to understand, because she contented herself with sitting at the table peacefully, sipping on a cup of steaming coffee.

When Megan had finished her breakfast, she sat and stared at her empty plate for a few moments. She couldn't stand not knowing any longer, and she looked up at Mrs. Mavilyn. Mrs. Mavilyn didn't give Megan a chance to ask her question.

"I heard news this morning that Nicholas is in a stable condition, but the doctors want to keep him in the hospital for a few days to monitor him," Mrs. Mavilyn said as she set down her cup.

Megan was relieved to hear the news, and she let go of the napkin that she had been quietly wringing in her lap. But she was astonished as well. It was as if the older woman had read her mind and had known exactly what she wanted. Mrs. Mavilyn smiled at the look on Megan's face.

"When you get to be as old as I am, Megan, you'll find that you develop a strong sense of things." Megan thought she caught a sparkle in Mrs. Mavilyn's eyes. "But something tells me that you already have a strong sense of things."

Megan thought about Mrs. Mavilyn's words. She had been discovering that her intuition was quite strong, and it seemed to be growing stronger by the day as Megan learned to trust it. Even the intense dreams that she had at night seemed to alert Megan often to things that might come to pass in the future. Megan didn't understand why she had this ability, especially since she sensed that this was not the case for most of the people around her.

Mrs. Mavilyn sighed and looked over at the fire. "If there was one thing my late husband Charles taught me, it was that it's all right to be a little different." She chuckled softly. "Lord knows, I got my share of oddities when the cards were dealt." Mrs. Mavilyn turned back to Megan and squeezed her hand. "Always remember to have faith in yourself, Megan," she whispered. "It's the greatest gift you can give yourself, and it can carry you into wondrous places that you've never dreamed of."

The Charm Tree

Megan smiled and would have replied, but presently, the kitchen door flew open with a bang, and a very sleepy-eyed Blaise tottered into the room, followed closely by a yawning Jared. Moments later, Helena entered with extremely frizzy hair. When Blaise caught sight of her, he pretended to be in shock and fell to the floor, writhing.

"Ahhh!—It's the bride of Frankenstein!"

It was far too early in the morning for Helena to retaliate properly, so she simply shot Blaise an acidic look—a look that meant she would get even with him later.

Everyone laughed. Blaise could always illuminate a room with his fiery, fun-loving spirit.

"Have a seat, kids," said Mrs. Mavilyn. "A round of rainbow pancakes and cups of hot chocolate coming up!"

The cook entered the kitchen soon after, and as the two women busied themselves with the cooking, the children sat around the table, joking and laughing in front of the fire. Megan's heart felt lighter, like a boulder had suddenly been kicked off of it.

The next few days at school seemed to pass by in a haze. Megan rushed home everyday to hear the news about Nicholas. Her mother always did her best to give Megan a comforting smile as she gave the same reply: Nicholas was still in the hospital, but she was sure he was going to be all right, and he would be home soon.

Megan's parents thought it was a good idea for her to go to the mountains with the other children to visit Mr. White Bear, even though Megan had insisted she stay home in case Nicholas was brought back from the hospital.

"It'll be good for you to get away for a while, Bumble Butt," her father had said. "Go and have fun; go tobogganing and make snow demons. We'll *all* be here waiting when you get back," he had added before messing up her hair playfully.

So, on the last day of school before Christmas break, the children hurried home to pack their things. Megan changed and threw her wet school clothes in the dryer as Lacy had *accidentally* knocked her into a huge snow bank during the afternoon break.

Megan was making a last plea to her parents to stay home as they ushered her and Blaise toward the front door to meet Baxter.

"Have a good time, honey," her mother said as she kissed Megan on the cheek.

Blaise rolled his eyes in disgust as Aunt Dolly wrapped layer upon layer of winter clothing on him. "Stay warm, Sweet Cheeks," she said and chuckled as she pushed Blaise

The Charm Tree

out the door. He almost rolled down the steps in his bundle of clothes.

Helena and Jared were waiting excitedly outside of the black Cadillac as Baxter loaded Megan and Blaise's bags into the trunk.

"You'll have loads of fun, Meg," said Jared reassuringly as he opened the car door for her.

"Thanks, I'm sure I will," Megan responded with a shy smile.

As the children piled into the car (Blaise needed a little help getting through the door), and they pulled away from the curb, Megan rolled down her window and shouted to her waving parents, "I'll be home before Christmas—I promise!"

During the long trip on the winding roads up through the mountains, the children amused themselves by playing card games and telling each other bizarre stories and jokes.

"Hey, did you hear about the stupid tap dancer?" Blaise asked. "He fell in the toilet!...No wait—he fell in the sink! Ha ha! Get it?"

After a long and unsuccessful search through all of Blaise's discarded winter clothing for Jared's video game console, the children decided it was snack time, and they pulled out a basket of food that Mrs. Mavilyn's cook had prepared for them. Megan smiled as she saw the cheese sandwiches, cantaloupe, orange jube jubes and peach juice.

"Let me guess," she said, "only orange foods on Fridays?"

The others laughed as they all dug in eagerly.

Megan liked the view of the snowy mountains and the trees as they traveled on into the growing dusk. She thought the scenery looked beautiful and peaceful—the perfect place to escape her troubles. When Blaise and Helena got into yet another heated argument over whose turn it was to choose the radio station, Megan sighed and decided that she was in desperate need of an escape right at that moment.

"Mr. White Bear's home on the left," Baxter droned in his usual flat voice.

Megan looked out of her window and saw, nestled in amongst the snow-covered evergreen trees, a charming log house. Warm, yellow light shone out from the windows, and smoke rose up in thin wisps from the chimney. Megan thought it looked lovely, just like a scene out of a Christmas card.

As they drove closer, a tall, broad-shouldered man came out from the house and waited for the car to pull up. He was wearing a large, red parka and had long, grey hair

The Charm Tree

beneath his blue toque. Once the car had stopped, Helena and Jared jumped out and ran over to the man, who put his arms around them in a warm embrace. Even Blaise ran over in his snow pants and excessively long toque to receive a welcoming hug from the man.

As Baxter gathered the luggage, Megan walked over to join the rest, and the man beamed a wide smile down at her.

"You must be Megan," he said in a deep voice. "Welcome to my home. Let's all go inside; I've got some hot cider all ready."

Megan and the others grabbed their bags and stepped inside the house. Carpets covered the wooden floor, and a cushy sofa and two armchairs were placed around an inviting fireplace. A festive Christmas tree stood before a very large bay window, which looked out over an enchanting winter scene. As Megan looked up, she saw a winding staircase that led to a loft overlooking the living room. It certainly wasn't as grand as Mavilyn Mansion, but Megan thought the log home was wonderful.

Everyone took off their coats and hats and hung them on hooks near the door. Helena, Jared and Blaise ran over to grab seats near the fire. As Megan followed them into the living room, she noticed some beautiful paintings of wildlife on the walls, and she spotted some interesting-looking objects on a bookshelf near the window. She walked over to investigate further and saw that they were intricate, wooden carvings of different animals. There were some geese, a fox, a beaver and a caribou. As Mr. White Bear entered the room carrying a tray of hot ciders, Megan noticed a charming figure of a large, white bear. She picked it up to get a closer look.

"I see you've found my namesake," Mr. White Bear said as he set the tray of steaming cups on a table in front of the others and walked over to Megan.

Megan looked up at him, puzzled.

"That is the spirit bear; it lives here in British Columbia. It's my spirit animal, and that's how I got my name," he explained. But you can call me Sam if you like."

"What's a spirit animal?" Megan asked as she too sat down and took a cup of hot cider.

It was Jared who answered. "Everyone has a spirit animal. It's a spirit who watches over you and gives you guidance in your life."

"What's my spirit animal?" Blaise asked as he rubbed at some hot cider he had spilt on his shirt.

Mr. White Bear chuckled and sat down in a large, leather armchair. "Only you can discover what your spirit animal is, Blaise. Though I have a feeling it may be a rather mischievous creature."

Helena sat up straighter and promptly nodded her agreement.

The Charm Tree

"There are spirits all around us," continued Mr. White Bear, "even in the trees."

Megan gazed out the large window at the snow-covered trees. "Spirits in the trees..." she whispered to herself.

Megan found Mr. White Bear fascinating. She discovered that he had painted the pictures on the walls and had carved all of the lovely wooden animals. He had made a living by selling some of his artwork to people all over the country. Megan could see why his work would be in demand; Mr. White Bear was a very talented artist.

Throughout the evening, Mr. White Bear told the children many interesting stories about the goings-on of the forest. He spoke of a herd of elk that lived in the area, and in the fall he had saved a hare, who had gotten his foot caught between some rocks. He showed Megan a scar of teeth marks on his left hand.

"That's what he gave me for my trouble," Mr. White Bear explained and chuckled.

Finally, as the fire began to burn low and eyelids began to droop, Mr. White Bear suggested it might be time for bed. Megan and Helena laid out sleeping bags near the dying fire, while Jared and Blaise chose to sleep in a room in the loft.

As Megan felt herself drifting off to sleep, she became vaguely aware of a sound that seemed to come from outside of the bay window—a sound like wings fluttering and faint whisperings.

"Only dreams..." Megan told herself before falling into a deep and comfortable sleep.

The next morning the children awoke late to bright sun on sparkling snow and hot food in the frying pan. As the children hungrily ate their breakfast of eggs, bacon and toast, they made plans for what they would do that day. Blaise and Jared wanted to make a snow fort, while Megan and Helena wanted to go skating. The children compromised by choosing tobogganing instead.

"Just remember, stay on the hills close by, and come back before it starts to get dark," Mr. White Bear said.

"We know, Grandpa," Helena and Jared said in unison as the children bundled up in their winter clothes. Out into the deep snow they trudged and around the side of the house to a wooden shed. There, they found some sleds, a wooden toboggan and a large, rubber tube.

After hours of sledding, snowball fights and making outrageous snow men (one had two heads and eight arms), the children fell down into the snow, laughing. Megan was having the best time playing with her friends amidst the seemingly endless white, mountain peaks that surrounded them.

The Charm Tree

"Should we go inside now?" Jared suggested.

"I'm ready to go back," Megan answered, and Helena started to rise.

Blaise, however, had spotted a large hill off in the distance, and his eyes lit up. "Just one more hill!" he said with enthusiasm.

"I can't climb up another hill," complained Helena, who let herself fall backwards into the snow, exhausted.

"That seems a little far," said Megan. "Are we allowed to sled on those hills?"

"Where's your sense of adventure?" asked Blaise as he got up and grabbed a large toboggan. "I say one more hill, then we can go in."

The others dragged themselves up and followed Blaise into the western sun. After a long and arduous climb up the hill, the children stood at the top, panting, and looked back down.

"Nope, not that side," Blaise said. "This side," he added as he began to walk the short distance towards the other side of the hill." The other children followed Blaise.

Megan's heart began to beat faster as she gazed down the steep and bumpy slope.

"I'm not so sure about this," said Jared; "It looks dangerous."

Even Blaise's eyes widened at the sight of the treacherous slope.

"I'm not afraid," Helena said in a sweet voice as she looked at Blaise and started to swing her blue scarf in circles, apparently daring him to go through with his plan.

Blaise wasn't about to admit he was wrong to his friends, especially after Helena's obvious challenge. Thus, after a moment's pause, Blaise said, "It'll be fine. All right, everybody on!"

Blaise got onto the toboggan first, and the other children climbed on after him. Blaise pushed off hard with his feet, and they were soon flying down the steep incline at an alarming speed. Helena screamed as they nearly hit a fir tree, and Megan almost flew off the back of the toboggan when they sped over a particularly large bump.

Blaise tried desperately to keep the toboggan travelling straight, but it kept veering off to the left, almost as if it had a mind of its own. As the toboggan sped down the slope, Blaise's eyes widened as he spotted a ledge, over which was another steep drop. The children were heading straight for it.

"Hold on!" Blaise cried as the toboggan sped over the ledge at full speed. All four children screamed as they flew into the air and landed down with a crash. Megan's toque fell down over her eyes as they raced down the new slope. After a few more terrifying bumps, she was able to push

The Charm Tree

her toque up just in time to see the toboggan enter what appeared to be an ice tunnel. The toboggan showed no signs of slowing down as it raced around bend after icy bend, the children's loud screams echoing on the glass-like walls of the tunnel. Suddenly, there was nothing beneath them, and the toboggan and children came crashing down into a patch of deep snow.

★ 8 ★
Wynterwyn

Megan pushed herself up and wiped the snow from her face. She was sure she had broken something. Sure enough, she had. Megan picked up a piece of the toboggan, which had been lying beneath her, and she threw it aside. Slowly, the others pushed themselves up into sitting positions and looked around at each other.

"Yeah! That was the ride of the century!" cried Blaise, his voice echoing against the high, icy walls of the tunnel. The others looked at him in disbelief. Everyone seemed to be okay, except for a few bruises and sore muscles, but they were still in shock from what had happened.

"This is all your fault, Blaise!" spat Helena, who was attempting to brush the snow out of her hair. "If only you could have steered properly!"

Megan looked up and saw, high above them, an opening in the tunnel that seemed to let in the last of the late sunlight. "Where are we?" she asked.

"I don't know," answered Jared. He stood up and tried to climb up the steep drop over which they had just fallen, but he quickly came sliding back down. "Well, it's pure ice," he concluded with dismay. "We definitely can't go back up the way we came."

"What do we do now?" Megan asked. "It'll be dark soon, and your Grandpa warned us about staying out after dark in the mountains."

"I guess we'll have to keep following the tunnel down and see where it leads," Jared answered.

The children got up and made their way tentatively over the ice. The swishing sounds of their snow pants and coats echoed through the vast tunnel. Megan got a queer feeling from the place; it was unlike anywhere she had ever been.

There seemed to be no end to the tunnel, and they were losing light with every bend they followed. The children turned a sharp corner, and they found themselves facing a new tunnel that branched off to the right from the one they had been following.

"Now where do we go?" asked Blaise.

His question was soon answered for him. A low, rumbling noise came from the tunnel on the right, and

The Charm Tree

the floor of the tunnel started to vibrate with the sound of heavy footfalls. There was no time to run. The children looked up in paralyzed horror as a huge and hairy white head emerged out of the darkness of the tunnel and looked at them with big, grey eyes.

With a long and shrill scream from Helena that seemed to reverberate throughout the entire mountain, the children began to run down the tunnel they had been following, no longer heeding the ice or the growing darkness. After a few bends in the tunnel, the children found themselves slipping on a steep incline and sliding down on their rear ends. Around a last curve they slid before landing down into another pile of soft snow. A cool breeze was suddenly on their faces, and high above them, the stars twinkled brightly in a purple and blue sky.

After only a moment's pause, the children were up and running again down a snowy slope towards a large snowdrift, behind which they fell down, panting.

"What was that thing?" Jared asked between heaving gasps.

"It must have been a spirit bear," said Megan, whose heart was racing.

"It didn't look like a spirit bear to *me*!" Helena replied.

Blaise stood up and peered out from behind the snowdrift towards the mouth of the tunnel. "Well, whatever it was, it doesn't seem to have followed us."

The children heard a growl from behind them, and they whipped around.

"What was that?" Blaise asked.

The growl turned into a low bark as Megan perceived a creature in the shadows between two spruce trees. Jared noticed it too.

"It's a dog!" he said in surprise.

"Where there's a dog, there must be people nearby," Helena said hopefully.

Blaise reached into his coat pocket and pulled out a gooey, orange jube jube from the day before, and he attempted to lure the dog with it.

"I don't think dogs eat jube jubes," Megan said skeptically. But to her surprise, the dog emerged from the shadows and made its way slowly towards them. It was a scruffy-looking creature with brown fur and a dirty, red handkerchief tied around its neck.

Blaise threw the jube jube into the snow just ahead of them. The dog approached carefully and sniffed the candy before picking it up with its teeth and eating it. Then it sat down, wagging its tail, and looked at the children expectantly, apparently hoping for more.

The Charm Tree

"What do you know?" said Jared in disbelief. "He likes it. Do you have any more, Blaise?"

Blaise rummaged through his pockets, but to no avail. The dog got up and started walking back towards the darkness of the trees. After a few steps, it stopped and turned its head back to look at the children.

"I think it wants us to follow it," said Megan.

"What have we got to lose?" Jared replied. So the children got up and started following the dog.

The moon came out from behind thick clouds and shone brightly, causing deep shadows amongst the trees and snowdrifts as the dog tramped on ahead through the forest. Megan looked up at the twinkling stars, which seemed to be particularly big and bright that evening. She had never seen a purple sky quite like that one before. The winter breeze on her face was cool and refreshing, and it seemed to whisper in the swaying tree branches.

As Megan looked closer at the trees, an odd sensation came over her. In the strange light created by the moon and the luminous snow, the trees almost seemed to take on human form, moving softly in the shadows. Megan shivered as she remembered something that Mr. White Bear had said the evening before: *There are spirits all around us, even in the trees.*

Megan gasped, and she stopped short. Had that been a person she had just seen, watching the children from the shadows? Megan blinked her eyes and peered out again, but all she saw were spruce and pine trees trailing far off into the distance.

"What's wrong?" asked Helena.

"Nothing," replied Megan. "I thought I saw something, but I must have been mistaken." All of Megan's senses seemed to be in overdrive in this strange forest.

"Well I think there *is* something wrong here!" Helena responded sharply and stamped her foot in the snow. "Doesn't anyone think it's odd that we're following a strange, dirty dog out into the middle of nowhere? I want to go home to Grandpa's and sit in front of the fire with a big cup of hot cider. And we're going in the wrong direction!"

"Come on, princess," Blaise responded. "It's not freezing out here or anything. In fact, I'm surprised at how un-cold it is with all of this snow and ice. And what do you have against the poor dog anyways?" Blaise asked as he gestured towards the wretched creature, who was now sitting in the snow with its head cocked to one side, observing the children interestedly. It appeared thoroughly unconcerned by Helena's remarks. "He can't help it if he's all dirty, being a forest dog and all. Can you boy?" Blaise added as he walked over to the dog, knelt down in the snow and started petting it. The dog jumped up with a

The Charm Tree

wagging tail and began licking Blaise eagerly all over his face.

Helena rolled her eyes with disgust and crossed her arms over her chest.

"I think we came halfway down the mountain," said Jared. "We can't get back up the way we came. Our only hope is to find somebody who can help us."

Just then, Megan spotted something glowing between the trees, a little off to the right, and she moved closer to investigate. The others noticed the light as well and followed Megan. The dog started to bark loudly, but Megan continued, and as she passed between two large spruce trees, she saw a strange and wondrous sight—a purple tulip growing right out of the snow, surrounded by a circle of glowing stones that looked like some kind of crystal. Megan became mesmerized by the beautiful flower and wanted to get closer, but just as her foot was about to pass within the crystal circle, the dog grabbed the seat of her snow pants in its teeth and pulled her back roughly.

Megan fell backwards into the snow and looked up at the dog in surprise. It was now standing over her with one paw on her chest. When she turned her head back to the place where the tulip had been, she saw only snow, sparkling in the moonlight.

"What happened?" Megan asked, perplexed and a little scared as the dog stepped aside and Jared helped her up.

"I don't know," answered Blaise with wide eyes, "but I think we should probably get out of here—fast! This place gives me the creeps."

"This place gives me the creeps," someone repeated and then giggled.

Blaise turned to Jared angrily, "Hey, are you making fun of me?" he asked with indignation.

"I didn't say anything," Jared responded innocently.

Helena looked around and shivered. "Let's keep following the dog," she said as she quickly led the others back out through the trees and underbrush to the path they had been following. Megan took a last glance back through the trees and thought she could see, once more, a glimmer of the strange crystals and flower.

The children moved on in silence, too afraid to say anything. They were all thinking of the creature they had seen in the ice tunnel and the mysterious flower that had vanished before their very eyes. They peered nervously into every shadow and jumped at every sound.

"I hope the dog gets us to where we're going soon; I'm so hungry," Blaise whispered to Megan. Megan heard his stomach grumble loudly. "And I gave him my last jube jube," Blaise added regretfully.

The Charm Tree

Megan had to agree. Not only had it been a very strange and tiring day, but she was also becoming more and more convinced that there was movement and whispers in the trees, and she had the growing suspicion that they were being followed.

Suddenly, the dog halted and lifted its leg onto a very large, old fir tree before passing around it. As the children followed a few moments later, they stopped short. The dog was nowhere to be seen, and there were no tracks to let the children know which direction it had taken.

"What the—?" said Jared.

"Now what do we do?" asked Helena with irritation.

Megan looked up and squinted. Was that smoke coming out of the top of the tree? She sighed and closed her eyes, leaning back against the trunk of the tree with pure fatigue. She wasn't sure of anything anymore. Suddenly, Megan was pushed forward roughly, as a door opened up right out of the bark of the tree, revealing a narrow staircase that seemed to lead down into the ground. Light and warmth poured out of the open doorway.

For a moment, the children just stared at one another, stunned into silence. They didn't know what they would find at the bottom of the staircase; all they knew was that they were famished and exhausted and wanted desperately to get in out of that strange, wintry night. So without a word, one after the other, the children descended the staircase, and the door swung shut behind them.

Amongst the trees, several paces off, a shadow that was darker than the others moved and faded into the forest.

Megan was first to enter into the small, candlelit room. A rough, wooden table stood in the centre with four chairs placed around it. Some shelves and cupboards had been built right into the rounded walls, and a large woodstove stood on the far side of the room. And there was the dog, sitting proudly and thumping its tail on the floor, with two people standing behind it.

An older man with a round face and thick sideburns stepped forward. "Jack just let us know we'd be havin' company tonight, and a company it is! What would four youngsters like yourselves be doin' out here?"

"We were tobogganing on the mountain, and we slid down into a tunnel of ice," Jared explained. "A large, hairy creature scared us out of the tunnel—that was when we saw your dog, and we followed him here."

"Did you, now? It looks like Jack has done his good deed for the day," said an old woman, who had a kindly face and was wearing a white hat with a matching apron.

The Charm Tree

She patted the scruffy dog behind his ears. "My name's Fiona, and this here is Shamus."

The older man nodded his head to the children.

Jared introduced himself and the others.

"Pleased to make your acquaintance," Fiona said. "We've just about got supper ready. Why don't you children take off your things and join us?"

Megan and the others knew it wasn't safe to stay with strangers, but the older couple seemed nice enough. The smells coming from the woodstove were very inviting, and they *were* starving. So the children said their thanks and hung up their outer clothing on some pegs on the wall. Jack walked over and lay down on what looked like a dirty pile of rubbish against the far wall, causing a big cloud of dust to rise in the process.

Shamus grabbed some extra chairs and told the children to take a seat at the table. Then he lit a pipe and sat down as well, while Fiona brought over some soup and steaming biscuits straight out of the oven. "This is moon mushroom soup," Fiona explained cheerfully. The children dove in hungrily. Megan thought the creamy soup was delicious, and she liked the moon-shaped mushrooms.

"Hey, it's glowing with a bluey-white light," Blaise said.

"Yup, there ain't nothin' like Fiona's cookin', even around here, and that's saying a lot," Shamus said with obvious pride.

Megan liked their funny accents. "Where are you both from?" she asked.

"Well, now," said Shamus, "we came over to Nova Scotia from Ireland about 1846 and started our own farm. It was a hard life, you know; the soil wasn't the same as good old Irish soil. Of course, the land in Ireland wasn't producin' much either at the time, so that's why we came." The children's jaws dropped. It had been well over a hundred and sixty years since 1846.

Shamus continued as if nothing was out of the ordinary. "One fine summer day, Fiona and I were walkin' through the fields with Jack, when we came upon this flower—unlike any flower we'd ever seen. In a ring of mushrooms, it was. Now, surely, Fiona and I know that it's mighty foolish to be steppin' into a ring of mushrooms, but the flower was so uncommonly lovely, and Fiona fancied it for her bonnet, so we stepped in just the same. Suddenly, we were here; Jack showed up moments later." Shamus sat back and took a long puff of his pipe.

The children became very excited. "We saw a flower just like that outside," Helena said. "It was in a ring of glowing stones. Megan was about to step into the ring, but Jack pulled her back."

The Charm Tree

Fiona brought over some hot tea and sat down. "Those flowers pop up from time to time. Jack doesn't seem to like them much," she explained. "Didn't like the trip over, I suppose, or maybe he just likes it better here and doesn't want to go back."

Megan felt the colour drain from her face. She set down her spoon and looked at the older couple. "And where are we?" she asked, her voice trembling slightly.

Shamus leaned forward. "Why, you're in Wynterwyn of course," he said before leaning back again and taking another puff of his pipe.

★ 9 ★
The Tree of Charms

"*Wynterwyn?*" repeated Blaise, who had some biscuit crumbs in the corner of his mouth.

"There's an echo in here!" bellowed Shamus. "Must be Cheswicks afoot," he added before throwing his head back and hooting with laughter. Fiona laughed too. Even Jack lifted his head from his dusty pile and cocked it to one side quizzically.

Blaise looked at Megan and mouthed the word "loonies".

"I've never heard of Wynterwyn before," said Jared.

"Neither had we," replied Fiona, "not until we got here, that is. But we sure enjoy it. It's always winter here, but we never seem to get a chill. Only beautiful skies and the land covered in sparkling, white snow. It's as winter should be in Wynterwyn."

"And except for those Cheswicks, who can be a pain in your backside when they choose to be, we're treated mighty fairly by the local people," added Shamus.

"Who are the Cheswicks?" Helena asked as she sipped her tea daintily.

"A thievin', meddlin' bunch of scallywags if you ask me," Shamus replied with obvious distaste. "But they don't do much harm, I suppose." He nodded to the dirty pile of rubbish Jack was lying on. "That's Jack's stash over there," he explained. "Jack disappeared for a time, and Fiona and I think he was with the Cheswicks down in their tunnels, becomin' just like them. When Jack returned, he brought back his stash a little at a time, and he guards it most fearsome."

"I'm just sure one of those Cheswicks went off with my favourite bumbleberry teapot," Fiona said with an irritated sniff as she refilled Blaise's empty plate. "I'd sure like to get my hands on one of them," she added, "but they appear and disappear like lightnin'. You hardly know they were there until they've gone."

Megan looked around the cozy kitchen and noticed two small doorways that appeared to lead into other rooms. "How did you come to live under a tree?" she asked.

The Charm Tree

"This room and the others were already dug out beneath this old, hollow tree when we got here," Shamus replied. "Must have been an abandoned Cheswick home, we figure, as they prefer underground livin'. But we fixed it up so that it was right livable. The way Fiona and I saw it, there was no reason *not* to live under a tree," he said matter-of-factly.

"Can you tell us how we can get back up the mountain?" asked Jared.

"From what I've been told, you can get back to where you came from by stepping into one of those flower rings," replied Shamus. "Then again, I've never tried it. Who knows where you might end up?" he added with a wink and a sly grin. Megan wasn't sure she liked the sound of that.

Fiona walked over to the counter and brought back a huge platter containing the largest doughnut Megan had ever seen. It was nearly the size of a tire and was chocolate with pink frosting and rainbow-coloured sprinkles. Blaise started to drool at the sight of it.

"Why don't you all stay in Wynterwyn for awhile?" Fiona suggested as she dished out the dessert. "You just might find you like it here."

As Megan tasted the dessert, she knew that she already liked Wynterwyn. She had never tried anything quite like the rich and moist, chocolate treat. The pink icing melted in her mouth like sugary clouds, and the sprinkles burst in her mouth like candy fireworks—each sprinkle having a flavour all of its own. As Megan looked around the table, she realized why the doughnut had to be so big. It seemed that no one could quite get their fill of it!

After dinner, the children leaned back in their chairs and sighed with sated contentment. Megan had never felt so full in her life. She watched as Fiona put down some leftovers for Jack—amazed that there *were* any leftovers after what the children had eaten. The scruffy dog jumped up eagerly to enjoy his dinner.

Megan became attracted to something in Jack's pile, which seemed to shine out and sparkle. She got up and walked over to investigate, but just as Megan reached out to pick up the shining object, Jack whipped around and growled at her fiercely with bared teeth. Megan jumped back in surprise.

"Hey there, not like that, girl," said Shamus. "You've got to do a trick for Jack before he'll give you somethin'."

"A—trick?" Megan said uncertainly.

"Sure," added Fiona. "Do somethin' that will amuse him, and Jack will give you a right nice treat. Go on, now."

Megan wasn't sure what she could do, but everyone was looking at her. Even Jack had abandoned his

The Charm Tree

dinner completely and had sat down, looking up at her expectantly.

Megan felt her face become red and hot. It didn't help when Blaise and Jared started pounding on the table chanting, "Let's go, Megan, let's go!" over and over again. Megan noticed her shadow on the wall, which the fire in the open woodstove had created, and she was reminded of something her father had taught her. Megan moved closer to the fire and put her hands together, twisting her fingers into strange contortions, and soon there was a flying dragon on the wall. Then there was a galloping horse, followed by a dog with a wagging tail.

Jack barked at that one, and everyone cheered. Megan laughed along with the others. Jack jumped up and started for the stairs.

"It looks like Jack's gift for you is outside, Megan," said Shamus. Would you children fancy a walk? The weather is always fine in Wynterwyn."

The children were not as afraid to go outside now that they were with the kindly, older couple, so they got up and put on their winter clothes again. Then up the stairs and out into the starry night they all went.

While Jack led the way through the forest, Shamus and Fiona spoke to the children about their duties in Wynterwyn.

"I do a bit of cookin' at Sharindra's palace," Fiona said. Helena perked up immediately at the mention of a palace. "Sharindra just loves my desserts," Fiona added happily.

"I'm the Palace Groundskeeper," Shamus explained proudly. "I look after the place, I guess you might say. And it looks like Jacky old boy might be leading us there right now."

Megan couldn't imagine what a groundskeeper would do in a land that's in perpetual winter, but it didn't take her long to find out. As they passed out of the trees and into a large clearing, the children stopped short and looked around in amazement. Under a bright, full moon, stood dozens of huge ice sculptures. Some were in the shape of animals, and others were creatures the children had never seen before. Some of the sculptures were funny geometrical shapes, and one was a castle large enough for a child to walk into. Each of the sculptures was crystal clear and perfect in its creation, glowing with the light of the moon.

"This is the Crystal Garden," Fiona explained breathily.

The children were speechless. They were in awe of the unearthly beauty that surrounded them.

Jack barked.

The Charm Tree

"It seems as though Jack has made another burglary," Shamus stated. "Even though this is not his garden to give, it would appear that he's givin' it to you anyhow, Megan."

Jack barked again.

"Ah, but only on full moons between the hours of nine o'clock and midnight, it would seem," Shamus added as the lines around his eyes crinkled in amusement.

Megan laughed. Jack walked over to her, and she bent down to scratch his ears.

"Did you make all of these sculptures?" Jared asked.

"Who me?" responded Shamus. "Nah. The Warfles made all of these", he explained as his right arm moved in a sweeping motion to take in the magnificent scenery. I just look after them."

"What's a Warfle?" Blaise asked, obviously amused by the situation. "Sounds like a bug or some kind of little, fuzzy creature—too small to make sculptures this big."

As Blaise was sniggering, a huge, white creature—much larger than a bear and walking on two legs—stepped out from around one of the nearby ice sculptures. It had a very hairy body with a large head and long arms that hung down by its sides.

"*That's* a Warfle," Shamus said as he put his hands in his pockets and sucked deeply on his pipe.

The children screamed and were about to run back into the forest before Shamus and Fiona stopped them.

"It's all right, children," Fiona assured them. "Kharn won't hurt you."

"The Warfles wouldn't hurt a fly, unless it was in self defense," Shamus explained as the children partially hid themselves behind the older couple and peeked out.

"I think we saw one of those in the ice tunnel," Megan said shakily.

"The Warfles do like their ice," Shamus explained. "They tend to wander a bit over the land, and you never quite know when to expect them," he added.

Jack walked over to the gigantic creature. It made a strange, guttural sound—somewhat between a bark and a growl—before bending down to pat Jack on the head with its enormous hand. Jack was nearly pushed down into the snow with the force of it.

The next thing the children knew, two lithe creatures were clambering up the back of the Warfle to settle onto its shoulders. Megan sucked in her breath upon first sight of them—they looked just like the statues outside of Mavilyn Theatre! The creatures were small and bony with large heads and ludicrous grins that stretched almost to their large, pointed ears.

Suddenly, Shamus lost his cheery demeanour. "And those would be Cheswicks," he stated flatly. Shamus

The Charm Tree

pointed to the creature on Kharn's right shoulder, "That one's called Winkler, and the other one would be Stinkler—two brothers who create more than their share of mischief."

As the children stared in amazement, Shamus continued, "The Warfles don't ever say much, but the Cheswicks never seem to shut up. Mind you, they only copy whatever you say most of the time. Gibberish it is."

"Shut up!" repeated Stinkler and then giggled into his hands.

All of a sudden, Helena lost her fear and walked out from behind Fiona. "Those are my ballet slippers!" she cried in indignation.

Blaise and Jared stepped out from behind Shamus for a closer look before hooting with laughter. True enough, the creature named Stinkler was sporting a pointed, brown cap; a grimy, green top; a brown pair of pants that were much too short for him; and…pink ballet slippers!

"Argh!" cried Helena.

"Do you want them back?" Megan asked tentatively.

The outrageous creature grinned stupidly before letting out a rather audible fart.

"No!" Helena answered quite firmly and crossed her arms over her chest.

"Hey, what's that light over there?" Jared asked, pointing to a colourful glow that could be seen over the treetops on the other side of the clearing.

"That would be the Charm Tree," Fiona answered, and she spoke with great reverence in her voice. "It starts to glow about this time of year."

"Charm Tree," repeated Winkler in a high-pitched voice before grabbing the ends of his pointed shoes. Kharn tilted his head back and bayed loudly.

The hairs on the back of Megan's neck tingled. For some reason the mention of the tree stirred something within her. Megan knew she had to see it.

"Can we go to it?" she asked.

"Of course we can," Shamus answered graciously.

So, with Jack in the lead once again, the group passed by the many wonderful ice sculptures and made their way to the far edge of the clearing. Even the gigantic Warfle followed with the two Cheswicks still perched on his shoulders. Megan noticed with interest that they seemed to be walking within a valley with high, white mountains surrounding them.

As they passed through the trees, the glowing light became brighter, and a faint tinkling sound could be heard. Megan felt an intense excitement building within her, and she had to fight hard to control it.

The Charm Tree

Once she had entered into a round clearing, her breath was completely taken away. There, before Megan and the others, stood a magnificent tree with smooth, silvery bark, and every vibrant hue you could possibly imagine shining out from its branches. The otherworldly light reached out to the surrounding ice sculptures, where it was refracted brilliantly and sent out into every direction. There was also a small, still pond within the clearing, which to Megan's surprise, was not frozen. This pond also reflected the strange, multi-coloured light upon its mirror-like surface. It was truly the most beautiful sight Megan had ever seen.

Just when Megan thought that the scene couldn't have become more miraculous, she caught sight of movement from the tree. Upon closer inspection, she spotted—lounging and dancing and dangling from the colourful branches—shining Fairies, hundreds of them! Megan soon realized that the tinkling sound that she had heard had come from the Fairies' wings beating on the tree branches.

"Oh, wow," breathed Helena, who was standing beside Megan.

Megan finally found her voice, "It's just like a magical—"

"—Christmas tree?" a voice from behind the children finished Megan's sentence.

Everyone turned to see a tall woman with long, dark hair and bright, brown eyes. She was wearing a flowing cape of rich, green velvet that was trimmed with white fur. Megan thought she looked just like a princess.

"Good evening," the woman said to the children. "My name is Sharindra; I welcome you to Wynterwyn."

The children found themselves speechless and could only stare at the lovely woman. Blaise's mouth was hanging open until Helena nudged him smartly in the ribs. Fiona took the liberty of introducing the children to Sharindra.

Sharindra smiled warmly. "I'm pleased to meet you all," she said. "I hope you are enjoying your time in Wynterwyn."

Helena was the first to respond. "Oh yes," she said, "We've never experienced anything so amazing!"

Sharindra moved closer to the Charm Tree. "You are very fortunate to be here at this time. There are few things in the universe as wonderful as this Tree," she said as she touched one of the branches affectionately; one of the tiny Fairies kissed her elegant finger.

"What is it?" Megan asked.

"No one knows exactly how the Tree came to be, but we have our legends," Sharindra explained with a smile. "What we do know is that a very powerful spirit inhabits the Tree. It grows charms that become ripe and begin to

The Charm Tree

glow at this time of year, and each charm contains a gift within it; all of the human babies that were born that year receive one. When the time is right, the Fairies each pluck a charm before being carried into your world on an enchanted breeze to deliver the charm to the baby who was meant to receive it."

Megan looked back at the Tree with increasing interest.

"Is it yours?" Blaise asked.

"Oh no," Sharindra replied and chuckled. "The Tree belongs to no one. I was merely appointed its Guardian."

A Fairy with flame-red hair and a sparkling, gold dress swooped down from one of the Tree's branches and landed on Winkler's head. Winkler had snuck down from Kharn's shoulder while the others had been talking and was attempting to steal one of the charms from the Tree. The Fairy shook herself briefly, causing gold dust to shoot out from her body. Winkler sneezed violently and fearfully scampered back up on to Kharn's shoulder. The Fairy giggled and flew nearer the children, zipping around them faster than the children could follow. The children laughed as they were bathed in glittering, gold dust.

"Children!" the Fairy chimed in a high-pitched voice.

"Yes, Dwindle," said Sharindra. "Children have come to visit the Tree."

"It smells nice here," Jared commented.

Megan had noticed the scent too. She knew she had smelled it at least a hundred times before, but she couldn't quite put her finger on it. It was a sweet smell, a soft smell, and Megan found it very comforting.

The Fairy named Dwindle swooped down to land on Jared's shoulder and fluttered her wings delicately. Jared stood awkwardly, not knowing how to react as the Fairy primped and preened her red locks, which fell down her back in tight ringlets.

Sharindra continued, "In two days time the people of Wynterwyn and our guests will have a great feast in celebration of the Tree. There will be entertainment, dancing, and of course, delicious food provided by Fiona." Sharindra turned and bowed graciously to Fiona, who flushed appreciatively and fidgeted with her apron. "I do hope you all will attend and stay as my guests in the palace."

The children looked at one another uncertainly. They hadn't planned on staying in Wynterwyn. Surely, Grandfather White Bear would be worrying about them and even now searching the mountain. They should be getting back as soon as possible. Sharindra seemed to read their minds.

The Charm Tree

"Wynterwyn is a very special valley," she said. "There are many different ways to enter our land, and once here, you may stay as long as you wish. When you decide to go home, all that is required is for you to step into one of the enchanted flower rings, and you will be returned instantly to your point of origin—at the time of your departure," she added with a meaningful smile. "You needn't worry about the people and engagements back home during your stay."

Sharindra's words seemed to erase instantly any concerns the children may have had.

"I'd love to see the palace!" Helena stated with excitement.

"It'd be awesome to go to the feast," Blaise added, already salivating.

Jared took the primping Fairy into his open palm, who began hopping playfully from finger to finger with obvious delight. "It would definitely be interesting to see more of your land and its people," Jared said to Sharindra.

Megan was staring at the Tree. "I'd like to stay," she stated simply.

"Splendid!" Sharindra exclaimed and clapped her hands. "Why don't you follow me, children, and I will take you to the palace.

The children thanked Shamus and Fiona for dinner. Then they turned and followed Sharindra out of the circular clearing and down a pathway through the trees. Fairies followed them, zipping from tree branch to tree branch, whispering and glancing curiously at the children.

Megan stole a quick glance back towards the Charm Tree. She knew it was the tree from her dreams, and she felt drawn to it, almost as if it were calling to her. Megan pulled out her crystal trinket from around her neck and held it tightly. Her father's stories *had* been true; there *were* mysterious creatures in the mountains and wonderful adventures to be had. Megan looked at the delicate, fluttering Fairies all around her and smiled. She wondered what her adventure had in store for her.

★ 10 ★
The Arrival of Special Guests

The children followed Sharindra out of the trees and soon found themselves staring up at a huge palace that shone brightly under the moonlight. The children were in awe of its grandness with its huge, arched doorway and its towers and spires reaching towards the sky.

"Is the palace made of ice too?" Jared asked.

Sharindra smiled. "No, it only looks that way. It's made from crystal that you can only find here in Wynterwyn. Please, come inside."

The children followed Sharindra toward the palace doors, which were guarded by two sleeping Cheswicks. As Sharindra approached, the Cheswicks jumped to attention and made rather unsuccessful attempts to look alert and serious about their duties. Megan had to stop herself from laughing aloud at their appearance. One of the Cheswicks had his helmet on crooked, and the other wore armor that was much too large for him. Sharindra appeared to take no notice, however, as the Cheswicks opened the palace doors and stood back to allow her and the children to pass through.

The children entered into a vast and wondrous hall that was lit by torches of purple flame. In the center of the hall was a large, crystal fountain, which sprayed water that seemed to be constantly changing color. Sharindra smiled at the looks of wonder and amazement on the children's' faces.

"I told you," she said, "Wynterwyn is a very special place."

"It *is* a very special place, and we'd like to keep it that way," said a voice from behind them. Everyone turned to see a tall and regal-looking man, who had wavy brown hair and wore an ornate, crimson-colored robe. Megan noticed that he had the same brown eyes as Sharindra, but his seemed to exude considerably less warmth at the moment.

"Children," Sharindra said, "I'd like you to meet my brother Varian. He lives here at the palace and helps me to protect the Charm Tree."

Jared held his hand out to greet the man, but Varian paid no notice as a tiny Fairy with blue hair and a purple

The Charm Tree

dress alighted upon his shoulder. Jared pulled his hand back awkwardly.

"I hope you all enjoy your brief stay in Wynterwyn," Varian said coolly. "We wouldn't dream of keeping you from your family and friends at this time of year." He smiled at the children, though Megan sensed that there wasn't much sincerity in his smile.

"I've invited the children to stay for the feast," Sharindra replied cheerfully. "I'm sure it will be particularly spectacular this year."

A little of the forced graciousness drained momentarily from Varian's expression. Soon enough, however, he had regained his cool composure. "I'm sure it will be," Varian said and gazed down at the children. "How lovely to have you as our guests. I will bid you all goodnight then. Come along, Trix," he said to the Fairy before turning and disappearing into a chamber at the other end of the hall.

"Varian is nervous about strangers in Wynterwyn," Sharindra explained. "Especially at this time of year. With the Charm Tree in bloom, we all must be extra vigilant in our duties."

"Why is that?" Jared asked.

"Not all of the beings in Wynterwyn have love for the Tree," Sharindra explained with sadness in her eyes. "Some see humans as terrible and dangerous creatures, who knowingly damage their own world and who might, in time, cause harm to our world. They would rather we had nothing to do with your kind and believe that the Charm Tree should be abolished."

Megan and the others were shocked. Everyone they had met so far in Wynterwyn had treated them with such kindness. Megan couldn't imagine how such a beautiful and enchanting land could contain people who felt this way.

Sharindra continued, "Long ago, some of the people from our valley decided to cut all ties with humans, and they moved to the borders of Wynter Land to form their own society. Some of the Fairies and Cheswicks went with them. Even a few of the Warfles, who are generally very kind-hearted and gentle, departed. It was a sad day for Wynterwyn," Sharindra said with downcast eyes.

"How do you know who you can trust?" Megan asked.

"Sometimes it's difficult to detect someone who has turned against us," Sharindra explained, "but if you look deeply into his or her eyes, you can always see the truth."

A shadow seemed to pass over Sharindra's face. "For others, the hatred in their hearts has grown to such an extent that they have begun to change physically, morphing into dark and ugly creatures."

The Charm Tree

A cold chill swept over Megan, and she shuddered. The children looked at each other with wide eyes and began to fidget uncomfortably. Megan felt deeply for Sharindra, who immediately changed her expression and attempted to look cheery again.

"But please don't concern yourselves, children," she said. "For ages upon ages the Charm Tree has stood safe and protected within the valley of Wynterwyn. We would never let any harm come to it or to our people. Now, I'm sure you all must be exhausted after such an eventful day. Allow me to show you to your rooms."

That night, as Megan stood in the beautiful room that she and Helena were sharing and looked out of her window, she marveled at the view. From her vantage point, Megan could see all of the palace grounds. There was Kharn, tirelessly carving his beloved ice sculptures, and just below, Megan could see Jack with the two Cheswicks who were guarding the palace doors. Megan laughed to herself. He really *was* a Cheswick dog. Her gaze moved to the Charm Tree, which glowed with its own special light under the starry sky. She couldn't understand how anyone would wish to harm it.

Megan changed into the nightgown Sharindra had provided and climbed into her cozy bed. Helena was already asleep soundly in her own bed across the room. Megan's thoughts drifted over the incredible events of the day before falling into a deep sleep.

Megan dreamed. She could see the Charm Tree glowing brightly ahead of her, and she ran towards it. This time, there was nothing to bar her way. Megan entered the circular clearing easily and looked around. There was no one there—no one to see what she was about to do. Megan's heart was pounding, and she was bursting with excitement as she reached her hand towards the Tree and—Megan heard a voice calling her name, and she fearfully whipped around.

"Megan, Megan, get up!" Megan slowly opened her eyes to see Helena kneeling on the edge of her bed, looking down at her.

"Get up!" Helena repeated excitedly. "There's a man down there, in the grounds; he's just arrived. Oh, you just have to see what he has with him!" Helena squealed with delight.

Megan got up and looked out of the window. She was amazed at the chaotic scene that was taking place just below her. What appeared to be half a dozen dragons were roaming about the grounds, easily escaping the frantic, armoured Cheswicks and Shamus, who were attempting to rein them in. The Warfles were trying desperately to protect their precious ice sculptures from the dragons'

The Charm Tree

fiery breath, while the Fairies zipped around, laughing and taunting the huge, scaly creatures. In the center of all of this madness stood a huge, muscular man with bright orange hair, who was laughing and bellowing out orders like he owned the place.

A few moments later, Megan heard the excited voice of Blaise in the hallway, and she knew that the boys had seen the newcomers as well.

"Woo hoo!" cried Blaise as he swung open the door to the girls' room, and he and Jared entered. They were already dressed in magnificent clothing. Jared wore black pants with a high-collared, sky-blue jacket that was decorated with silver embroidery. Blaise also wore black pants, but he was dressed in a loose-fitting, silky gold shirt with a bronze-coloured vest. He had even combed and smoothed his long, blonde hair.

"Do you see what's going on down there in the grounds?" Jared asked with wide eyes."

"Why, whatever are you talking about?" Helena said coolly before she sat down on the edge of her bed and pretended to examine her nails. "I see nothing of consequence down there."

"Are you *kidding* me?" Blaise asked incredulously. "Didn't you see the dragons?"

"Well, maybe we could if you would leave us in peace so that we can get dressed properly," Helena said as she pushed the spluttering boys back into the hallway and slammed the door."

"Come on, Meg, let's get dressed!" Helena said excitedly, and she ran over to a chaise longue and picked up a rose-coloured dress with puffy sleeves that was decorated with embroidered gold flowers. Megan laughed, "That dress is perfect for you Helena," she declared.

Megan walked over to the chaise longue hesitatingly, cringing at the visions of pink frills and flowy skirts that danced through her mind. To her surprise, however, Megan found a midnight blue, velvet tunic with matching leggings and a long, braided, silver belt with tassels. She thought the clothes were wonderful. Helena giggled as she found their matching shoes beside the chaise.

After Megan and Helena had changed into their new clothes, they joined the impatient boys in the hallway.

"Wow, you two look great," Jared commented as his twin twirled in her golden shoes, causing her skirt to swirl around her.

"You guys look nice too," Megan replied.

Helena stopped twirling. "Yeah, even Blaise cleans up kind of nice," she said with uncharacteristic approval.

Blaise's face flushed slightly as he quickly responded, "Whatever, let's go round up some dragons!" and they all ran down to the front hall and out the palace doors.

The Charm Tree

The children met Sharindra and Varian just outside the palace doors. Sharindra was attempting to look stern, considering the commotion that was taking place in her palace grounds, but she was barely managing to contain her amusement. Varian, on the other hand, looked appalled at the chaotic scene. Trix was fluttering near his head, shedding sparkling, purple dust in her agitation.

"This is a disgrace!" Varian spat. "Roarke must take control of those beasts!"

"I'm afraid he's doing his best," Sharindra replied and chuckled as the orange-haired man named Roarke attempted to grab the reins of a huge, golden-scaled dragon and yelled out as the impetuous creature burned him.

"You'll get ten whips for that, Nezdreg!" the man bellowed before he managed to subdue the dragon, which immediately pulled in its wings and lay down with its head bowed. Megan was impressed.

The large man, who was wearing a gold-coloured breastplate adorned with a red dragon and a leather tunic, turned and smiled pompously at Sharindra and the others. Mere moments later, however, a male Fairy shedding green dust swooped by, carrying a squirming—and rather unwilling—Cheswick beneath him, who inadvertently kicked the man in the head, sending him flying face down into the snow.

Megan was amazed that such a tiny Fairy could carry a full-grown Cheswick. She, along with Sharindra and the others, broke down into peels of laughter, while Varian, who was obviously horrified, turned and marched back into the palace with Trix fluttering close behind him.

As Shamus helped the man get back onto his feet, a booming cry and the sound of chiming bells was heard from above. The men, along with a few Cheswicks and a sleek, grey dragon, had to jump out of the way to avoid being trampled by a team of six flying white stags that landed down elegantly and came to a stop right in front of the palace doors. The stags, which were now blowing into the winter air and pawing the snow-covered ground, were attached to a silver sleigh, upon which sat a large man with a white beard. He was wearing a pale blue coat trimmed with white fur and a matching hat.

"Welcome, Fardymor," Sharindra said graciously as the man descended from the sleigh and walked over to take her extended hand.

"As always, it is a great pleasure to be here at your palace, Sharindra," the older man said. "I am very much looking forward to the feast and the Harvesting of the Tree."

Sharindra introduced the children and explained that they were guests from the Upper World. Fardymor

The Charm Tree

greeted them warmly. Megan thought the man seemed very distinguished and pleasant.

Roarke walked over to join them, looking disgruntled as he brushed snow off of his bare arms and legs and out of his small, pointed beard. Dwindle flew down and landed on his shoulder, where she began tickling his ear with her wings. Roarke swatted at her absentmindedly, while Fardymor patted him on his other shoulder.

"It's good to see you again, Roarke. How is the training going with the young dragons?" he inquired with an amused twinkle in his eyes. Most of the dragons were still ambling aimlessly around the grounds and snorting scorching flames from their nostrils, heedless of the frantic Cheswicks who were still attempting to gain control of them. Megan saw Winkler scrambling up a tree, trying desperately to escape the baby green dragon that was chasing him. Next to the white stags, which were standing patiently and waiting for their master, the dragons appeared positively unruly.

Roarke stood up tall and puffed out his large chest. "Dragons are a fierce and volatile race," he said with a deep voice, "but I feel confident that I can break this pack soon and bend them to my will."

"I'm sure you would have had them reined in and installed in the palace stables by now if I hadn't landed down with my team and scattered them," Fardymor offered charitably, amusement still crinkling the lines around his eyes.

"Too true," Roarke grunted. "Well, I'd best get at it. They've been flying all night, and they'll need some rest before the race later on."

"Race?" Blaise and Jared asked in unison.

"Every year on the day before the feast we have a race," Sharindra explained. "It's part of the festivities. Anyone can enter."

Blaise and Jared looked at each other, nearly beside themselves with excitement. "Can we help you with the dragons?" Jared asked.

"Of course," Roarke replied. "These Cheswicks are not well equipped to manage such savage creatures. Handling dragons requires courage and a firm command."

Blaise and Jared stared up at Roarke with obvious admiration. Megan found she couldn't watch as the boys followed the huge man back out into the bustling grounds. Even the smallest of the dragons stood taller than the boys.

"Well, I think I will take my stags to the clearing of the Tree and tie them up," Fardymor said. "They'll be content there, and it's probably best to keep them as far from the dragons as possible," he explained and chuckled merrily.

The Charm Tree

"Can I come with you?" Megan asked, surprising herself with her own boldness.

"Certainly," Fardymor answered graciously. "I would be delighted to have your company."

Helena chose to go back into the palace with Sharindra to see about breakfast, while Megan watched Fardymor remove the harness from his team and unhitch them from the sleigh. As the stags moved, tiny bells attached to leather collars around their necks chimed softly. When Fardymor had finished, Megan was surprised to see the creatures follow their master voluntarily towards the clearing of the Charm Tree.

Megan thought the stags were beautiful with their pure white fur and gentle eyes. As Fardymor began to tie the stags to some hitching rails around the outside of the clearing, Megan ventured as far as to pet one of them on the nose. To Megan's delight, the creature bent its head and nuzzled her.

"You have a very nice spot here," Megan said to it. "You can stand here and look at the Charm Tree all day." Megan turned and looked at it herself. It was still glowing with its unearthly light. Fairies were moving about its branches and whispering to one another, their fluttering wings tinkling on the charms. Fardymor finished his work and came over to stand beside Megan.

"It's marvelous, isn't it?" he said.

"Yes," Megan breathed.

"I come to the valley every year to witness the Harvesting and to play my part," Fardymor explained.

"Where are you from?" Megan asked.

"Wynterwyn is only one valley within our world," Fardymor explained, "although it is a very special valley of course. I come from another area of Wynter Land. A soft wind always blows over our pristine land of sparkling snow."

"Is my world very far away?" Megan asked.

Fardymor looked thoughtful for a moment and stroked his short, white beard. "I suppose you could say we're in a different place, but we share the same space," he replied. "The Charm Tree connects our two worlds, which are really only a breath apart."

Megan wasn't sure she understood, but she was bursting with questions. "Is Roarke from Wynter Land as well?" she asked.

"Heavens no," Fardymor replied and chuckled. "He can't stand the snow, I'm afraid. He comes from Summer Land, a part of our world where the sun shines brightly every day and the flaming foxgloves are always in bloom."

Megan was astonished. This all seemed so unreal to her.

The Charm Tree

Fardymor continued, "Sharindra is from Summer Land as well. She made a very courageous sacrifice to leave her beloved home to come here and protect the Tree when those of our people who resented the humans separated. Sharindra, like most of us, feels love for your people and believes that a wondrous potential for greatness lies within each of you. You can become whoever you want to be. You can make your dreams come true, or you can create your worst nightmare. There is no limit to your power, and your fate lies in the choices that you make," Fardymor said as he looked down at Megan warmly.

Megan felt inspired by Fardymor's intense words. She had never thought of herself or her life quite like that before. In that moment, she felt like she could create whatever she wished, and she knew what her deepest desire was. Megan thought of Nicholas as she looked back at the Charm Tree and the shining Fairies. "How do the Fairies know which charms to deliver to the babies?"

"The Fairies have a very special bond with children from your world, Megan," Fardymor explained. "They know instinctively which charm is meant for each child."

Megan walked over to the Tree and touched a particularly attractive charm with gold light shining from its core. It felt warm and firm to her touch.

"That one is the gift of music", Fardymor explained. He reached up and pointed to another charm with a deep blue light. "And this is the gift of scientific understanding."

Megan touched another charm with a beautiful, emerald green glow.

"That one is the charm of healing," Fardymor explained. "It is a very special gift."

Megan looked at the charm with growing interest. "The charm of healing," she repeated to herself.

Fardymor noticed the trinket around Megan's neck, and sadness seemed to come into his eyes. "It would seem that this particular charm didn't get delivered."

Megan touched her crystal with astonishment. "My father found this in the mountains when he was a boy. There was an injured Fairy nearby," she explained.

Fardymor nodded knowingly. "Sometimes those who have separated achieve small victories," he explained. Megan looked down at her charm sadly.

Fardymor changed his expression and said, "Well, I don't know about you, but I'm famished, and I think the stags are too." At this, the white stags became restless and began to paw at the ground. "I think I will ask the workers in the stables to bring over some food for them before heading back to the palace to enjoy some of Fiona's famous cooking. Will you allow me to escort you to breakfast, Megan?" Fardymor asked graciously.

The Charm Tree

"Thank you," Megan replied with a smile and took the arm that Fardymor offered her. As they were leaving the clearing, Megan stole a last glance at the glowing, emerald green charm. She remembered the dream she had had the night before, and an idea began to take root in her mind.

★ 11 ★
A Shining Treasure is Captured

Breakfast in the palace was an extravagant affair for the Wynterwynians and their guests. Fiona explained to the children that they had their choice of pipsqueak pancakes or bluebell waffles smothered in her special syrup or dragon eggs prepared any way they wished. There were fried moon mushrooms, fritter nuts, cheese swirls and hot tickleberry bread straight out of the oven. Dozens of platters of fruit the children had never seen before covered the tables, and steaming, pink porridge filled numerous tureens. Fiona also offered the children bumbleberry juice or rainbow root tea to drink.

With all of these wonderful dishes to choose from, Megan was horrified and embarrassed when Blaise requested a bowl of butterscotch pudding to go along with his poached dragon eggs and huge stack of bluebell waffles. Roarke slapped Blaise heartily on the back and praised him on his healthy appetite. "You've gotta eat if you want to work with dragons!" Fiona happily whisked herself away to the kitchen. In a flash, the cheerful cook was back, and she produced not only a huge batch of pudding, but a few pans of chocolate mud pies as well.

Jared leaned over his plate of tiny pipsqueak pancakes and fritter nuts and whispered to Megan, "If this is breakfast, I wonder what the feast will be like tomorrow." Megan could only imagine; she decided that Fiona must be using magic to produce all of this wonderful food so quickly.

After breakfast, the children went out into the palace grounds. They passed the morning by walking around and looking at all of the enchanting ice sculptures. When the children had reached the ice castle they had seen the night before, they eagerly began to investigate it further. They discovered within its icy walls a pulley system that could close the castle gate as well as a staircase that led up to a second level. Here, the children could stand on the turrets and throw snowballs down on unsuspecting passers-by. Winkler and Stinkler got several facefulls of snow before Kharn arrived, and they were able to climb up onto his huge shoulders. Kharn was nearly as tall as

The Charm Tree

the castle, and with him arming the Cheswick brothers with ample amounts of ammunition, the children soon had to surrender and retreat, laughing, into the safety of the castle.

After lunch, the children went with Roarke to the palace stables to check on the dragons. There they found Varian, who appeared to be inspecting the gates of the stalls. When he saw Roarke and the children approaching, he immediately stopped what he was doing and assumed a regal bearing.

"Just making sure they can't escape," he said to Roarke disdainfully.

"You'd like my dragons if you gave them a chance, Varian," said Roarke. "I've trained them well. Why don't you take one of them out for a ride?" he asked with a slight glint in his eyes. Just then, the baby green dragon that was in the nearest stall sneezed and sent a thin, scorching flame through the open bars of the gate. Varian had to jump back ungracefully to avoid having his cape start on fire. Roarke and the boys broke down into howling laughter. Even Megan and Helena had to hide their amusement with their mittened hands.

Varian was outraged. "Keep those creatures away from me!" he yelled at Roarke, whose laughter followed the humiliated man out of the stables.

The children remained to help Roarke feed the dragons. Roarke explained that the feed was a mixture of sun blossoms and stink weed, and the children had to plug their noses as they threw handfuls of it into the dragons' stalls, all the while being careful not to get too close. Sometime later, Sharindra entered the stables and announced that the race would be taking place shortly. "If you would like to enter, you had better choose your ride," she said to the children.

Roarke muzzled a few of his best dragons so that they couldn't harm anyone, and the children helped him lead the creatures out into the yard. There they found a huge group of Wynterwynians congregated outside of the palace. A line of Fairy dust had been sprinkled on the snow, and Shamus stood nearby holding a large, crystal bell. Fiona called and waved to the children from her spot near the palace doors, while Varian stood beside Sharindra with his arms crossed and a look of utter distaste on his face. The children heard the sound of chiming bells and turned to see Fardymor, who was approaching with a selection of stags from his team.

Roarke helped Blaise and Jared mount onto the dragons of their choice before choosing a rather fierce-looking dragon with red scales for himself. Winkler and Stinkler hopped up onto the back of a stag, while Helena and Dwindle whispered behind an ice sculpture of a

The Charm Tree

unicorn, obviously hatching a plot. Megan stood by with the other spectators.

"Aren't you going to race?" Fardymor asked Megan.

"I don't think so," Megan said, suddenly shy.

"Are you sure?" Fardymor asked as he brought over a beautiful white stag. Megan recognized it as the one she had been stroking earlier near the Charm Tree.

"His name's Kanter," Fardymor said. "Would you like to get on him and see how it feels? He won't let you fall."

Megan agreed reluctantly and let Fardymor help her onto the back of the stag. She felt unsure for a few moments, but as Megan grabbed onto Kanter's neck, and she sensed the confidence in the creature as it trotted over to join the others at the starting line, she began to lose some of her fear.

Helena approached the starting line in Fardymor's silver sleigh, which was pulled by none other than Dwindle. Blaise laughed derisively from atop his large, golden dragon. "Do you really think that Fairy can compete with dragons and stags?"

Dwindle began shedding gold dust angrily, while Helena simply sat up straighter with her nose in the air.

Megan noticed Trix fly over to Varian and whisper something in his ear before fluttering over to take her place at the starting line.

Sharindra stepped out in front and spoke to the contestants and crowd. "The rules of the race are as follows (Sharindra indicated a mountaintop in the distance from which shone bright, gold light in the growing dusk): You must fly to the top of that mountain and pass around the post with the gold stars. You must capture a star and then return here. The first one to cross the finish line is the winner. When Shamus rings the bell, you may begin."

Shamus stepped forward and yelled, "Good luck to all!" He was about to ring the bell when he noticed Jack, who had snuck up to the starting line carrying a small Cheswick child on his back. "Get out of there, Jack!" Shamus bellowed. "You know you can't fly." Jack scowled and trotted away.

Shamus rang the crystal bell. Stinkler farted and giggled as everyone took off in a flurry of pounding feet and Fairy dust. Megan felt a rush of fear as the stag beneath her began to gallop across the yard, and she cried out as it kicked off strongly from the ground and leapt into the air. Megan closed her eyes when she felt the cool wind rushing against her face.

Megan heard Jared cry out exuberantly, and she opened her eyes to an amazing sight. Jared was just to her right on a grey, female dragon with its wings flapping madly, while Trix was flying on Jared's far side. Blaise and Roarke were above Megan and slightly ahead on their

The Charm Tree

soaring dragons. Winkler and Stinkler were to Megan's left on their white stag, which was running in the air like Kanter. To Megan's surprise, Helena and Dwindle were not far behind her.

Megan relaxed and allowed herself to feel the thrill of flying through an evening sky that was quickly filling with bright stars, and she cried out joyously. Her stag snorted in response and flew even faster. Megan's heart was beating so fast with fear and excitement that she thought it might explode. "Yeah!" she cried and reached her right arm out as Kanter flew into the middle of a soft, purple cloud. Megan had never experienced anything so glorious and exhilarating in her life.

Too soon, Roarke yelled out, "Star post approaching!" as he swooped his dragon down. Megan looked down and saw the post on the top of the mountain, and it had a number of shining, gold stars attached to it. Kanter apparently knew what to do, as he dived down as well. Megan watched as both Roarke and Blaise flew their dragons close to the post and made a quick snatch for their stars. They had both succeeded and made a tight turn back in the direction of the palace. Winkler and Stinkler flew down on their stag, and Winkler was just able to catch his star by a single point. As the Cheswick brothers made a sharp turn around the post, Stinkler slipped off the back of the stag. Megan's eyes widened in horror, but a moment later, she spotted Stinkler holding onto the stag's short tail and trailing behind happily in the wind.

As Megan and Kanter neared the star post, Megan imagined that they must be near the borders of Wynterwyn by now. She reached out to grasp her gold star, and Megan spotted, far below her, some Warfles that were milling about amongst the trees. Upon closer inspection, Megan also caught the movement of Cheswicks hopping around in a clearing. She had little time to wonder about it once she had successfully grabbed her gold star, as she had to concentrate on holding tight to Kanter, whose body was already twisting to veer back towards the palace.

Once Megan felt secure again, she glanced behind and saw Jared swoop down on his dragon to catch a star. However, as he reached out towards the star post, Trix suddenly zipped right in front of his face, causing him to lose his balance. Megan screamed out as she saw Jared start to slip off of his dragon. The lithe, grey creature quickly changed position, allowing Jared to regain his balance. Trix claimed her star and quickly made for the finish line, while Jared and his dragon doubled back towards the star post, where Jared successfully grabbed his star.

Helena and Dwindle were not far behind Jared, and soon, Helena was cheering as she held up her gold star. Blaise twisted his body to look back and yelled out to

The Charm Tree

Helena, "Your star is bigger than your pixie—why don't you quit now and save yourself some embarrassment!" Roarke roared with laughter.

Immediately, gold dust began to shoot off from Dwindle's body. "Who are you calling a pixie?" she cried before pulling in her wings and diving up in Blaise's direction. When Blaise caught sight of the fast approaching sleigh, he panicked and veered his dragon straight into Roarke's red beast, causing them both to veer off course. The wing of Roarke's dragon hit Trix, who momentarily lost her wind and began falling down through the clouds. Dwindle zipped by them all and headed straight for the finish line. Megan cried out with joy as Dwindle and Helena landed down smoothly before the cheering crowd.

Moments later, Winkler and Stinkler landed down, with Stinkler still attached to the stag's tail, followed by Megan and Kanter. Jared arrived next on his dragon with Blaise, Roarke and Trix trailing in last. Trix, who was angrily shedding purple dust, flew directly into the palace. Roarke was still laughing, while Blaise had a stupefied look on his face.

Sharindra congratulated Helena and Dwindle, and she presented each of them with a small, gold star on a chain. Winkler, Stinkler and their stag each received silver stars, while Megan and Kanter were awarded blue stars.

Dwindle looked slightly humorous carrying the chain (which was much too big for her) around her neck as she flew past Blaise's head proudly.

During the commotion of the aftermath of the race, Megan snuck away from the crowd and walked Kanter back to the clearing, where she tied him to the hitching post. "Thanks," she whispered to the stag as she stroked his nose.

Megan turned to look at the Charm Tree. Except for the stags, the clearing seemed to be empty. Megan could no longer see movement within the Tree nor hear the usual soft, tinkling noise. It seemed that even all of the Fairies had left to watch the race. Megan walked closer to the Tree and looked at the glowing, green charm with wide eyes. She could take the charm now, just like in her dream, and no one would know. After the feast tomorrow, she could return to her own world with the others and give the charm to Nicholas. Then he would never have to be sick again.

Megan took a last anxious look around the clearing before she reached up and plucked the shining treasure from its branch. It glowed brightly in her hand. The stags began to paw at the ground and snort nervously, and the water in the nearby pool began to ripple, but Megan paid no notice. She quickly wrapped the charm inside of her scarf and tucked it inside of her coat. Being careful not

The Charm Tree

to look in Kanter's direction, Megan walked swiftly from the clearing to rejoin the others, who were entering the palace for the victory dinner.

Megan entered the hall and stopped before the crystal fountain to watch its colorful waters splash into the pool below. It was then that Megan noticed an inscription etched into the fountain base:

> Live each day with a giving heart
> Treasure, from you, will never part
> Pine away in miserly gloom
> Justice will come to seal your doom

Megan's heart plummeted as she read the words. It wasn't such a bad deed, what she had done, Megan told herself. She had taken the charm for Nicholas, so she *was* living with a giving heart. Presently, Jared approached from behind and patted Megan on the shoulder, causing her to jump.

"Sorry," he said, "I didn't mean to scare you. I just wanted to congratulate you on winning third place in the race," he said.

"Thanks," Megan said weakly. A tinge of guilt stirred within her, and she felt that perhaps she wasn't deserving of Jared's praise just at that moment. But Megan told herself that her unease was only due to the race—it had been Dwindle's doing that she received third place, not her own racing ability.

"Are *you* ok?" Megan asked. "I saw you nearly slip off of your dragon up there."

"Oh, yeah," Jared replied, his face turning red. "That purple Fairy sure doesn't know how to fly well," he said before moving over to the tables that had been set up in the hall.

Megan pondered Jared's words for a moment before running up to her room to take off her coat. She took the glowing charm out of her scarf and hid it beneath her pillow. Then Megan walked to the window and looked at the Charm Tree below. There were countless charms on the Tree, Megan told herself. Surely one small charm wouldn't be missed. Then Megan looked down at the charm her father had given her, and she remembered Fardymor's sad eyes. *This one hadn't been delivered.*

Megan pushed the thought from her mind and returned to the hall to celebrate with the others. She was doing what was best for Nicholas, and that was all that mattered, she told herself. Megan grabbed a goblet of Fiona's shimmering cider and toasted Helena and Dwindle with the others before sitting down to a delicious meal of dragon breath stew and dewdrop dumplings.

★ 12 ★
A Dark and Dreadful Deed

The next morning Megan awoke to bright sunlight shining through her window. She glanced over at Helena, who was sleeping soundly with the gold star still around her neck. Megan checked that the charm was under her pillow; sure enough, it was safe and sound, shining brightly with its emerald green glow.

Megan walked over to the window and looked out. It was the day of the Harvesting of the Charm Tree, and the Wynterwynians were already busily putting up festive decorations. The Cheswicks placed decorations on the trees, the Warfles helping with the higher branches, and the Fairies were flitting about, hanging garlands and sprinkling their magical dust everywhere. Megan thought with delight that the scene below her looked like a true winter wonderland.

Megan dressed herself in her beautiful Wynterwynian clothes and went down to the hall, where the tables were being set and decorated for the evening's festivities. When Megan entered the vast room, she nearly ran straight into Varian, who to Megan's surprise, seemed to be in a pleasant mood. Varian even teased Megan about the need to watch where one is going before he sauntered out of the hall, whistling.

Megan walked to a table, where Sharindra and Fardymor were enjoying their breakfast, and sat down.

"Good morning, Megan," Sharindra greeted cheerfully. "Would you care to have some bubble pancakes? Daisy has just whipped some up."

"Thanks," Megan said as she accepted the plate that Sharindra offered her gratefully.

"Are you excited about the Harvesting?" Fardymor asked.

"Oh yes," Megan replied. "I'm sure we have nothing like it in our world."

"There's nothing quite like it in *any* of the worlds," Fardymor replied with a smile.

Megan was reminded of something. "Sharindra, back home I saw some statues that look just like Winkler and

The Charm Tree

Stinkler. One time, I thought I saw one of them wink at me, and another time, the statues were gone altogether."

Sharindra chuckled and glanced at the Cheswick brothers, who were even now stealthily removing silverware that Fiona had just placed on a table. "If you can enter our world, Megan, it only makes sense that people from Wynterwyn can enter your world as well. Sometimes, when humans have seen someone from our land, they create a statue or likeness of what they saw. That person or creature can then use the statue to easily go into and out of your world.

"Oh," Megan replied as she too watched the mischievous creatures.

"I do hope they didn't cause too much trouble," Sharindra said weakly as Fiona caught Winkler attempting to replace some blue roses in a vase with dried stinkweeds and angrily shooed the brothers from the hall.

"Only the usual," Megan replied and laughed.

Presently, Helena and the boys entered the hall and sat down at the table. As Fiona hurried over to help dish out their breakfasts, Blaise amused everyone with a dream he had had of sailing a huge ship over high seas and battling with sea monsters.

"So I jumped onto his head with my sword, and down into the inky depths we dived…!"

After breakfast, Helena suggested they visit the stags and the Fairies near the Charm Tree. Megan wasn't sure she felt like going back there just yet, but Helena insisted upon seeing Dwindle, so the children walked out into the bright sun and sparkling snow and headed towards the circular clearing.

Once there, the children were surprised to find that they were not the only visitors in the clearing. An old woman was standing beside the rippling pool of water, which was reflecting the multi-colored glow from the Tree. The woman had long, grey hair and olive-coloured skin, and she wore a pale green gown.

Upon a closer look at the pool, Megan was delighted to see tiny figures diving in and out of the water and dancing across its shining surface playfully. They had strange bodies that were almost transparent and which seemed to be reflective, like the pool itself. As Megan gazed at the frolicking figures, she thought she could almost hear their laughter in the splashing and bubbling of the water. The other children seemed amazed by the scene as well.

"Who are you?" Blaise asked the woman with a shocked look on his face.

The woman raised her eyebrows. "I was about to ask you the same thing, young man," she replied sternly.

The Charm Tree

"We apologize for our friend's rudeness," Helena replied before sending Blaise a scathing glance. Then she adopted a superior manner and proceeded to introduce herself and the others.

"I'm happy to meet you," the woman stated. "My name is Nerrivik; I've come for the Harvesting of the Tree."

"How did you get here?" Jared asked, looking around hopefully for some sign of a dolphin or a giant sea horse.

Nerrivik chuckled, apparently reading Jared's mind. "I came through the pool," she replied as she gestured towards the colorful, rippling water.

The children stared. "How is that possible?" Blaise asked. "You're not even wet."

"It's a very unique pool," Nerrivik explained, "and I have a deep connection to the water. I watch over the creatures and spirits of the water."

The children looked down at the pool with its skipping and diving water sprites. Megan began to feel a strange sensation growing within her as she looked deeply into the water. Something began to take shape.

"What do you see?" Nerrivik asked Megan calmly.

Megan was amazed to see a white, elegant shape take form in the water right before her eyes. It fluttered its wings gently and unfurled its long, graceful neck. Two sprites eagerly jumped onto its back and giggled. "It's a swan," Megan breathed in wonderment. The sight of it gave Megan a feeling of peace and comfort.

Nerrivik smiled. "That's your spirit animal," she explained. "The swan is a guide for you when you feel lost or afraid, and you carry its essence within you. It's reassuring to know that wherever you go, you are never alone."

Megan pulled out from her coat pocket the card that the Gypsy woman had given her back in Shansymoon and smiled at the beautiful image of the swan. Could she have known? Megan thought to herself.

Helena moved closer to the pool eagerly and peered down. Instantly, a large, brown shape began to emerge with a bright, furry mane. Huge jaws opened in a silent roar to reveal big, pointed teeth. Several sprites scampered and dived deep into the pool. "A lion!" Helena squealed with delight.

"Good going, sis!" Jared cried.

"How about you?" Nerrivik asked, looking at Jared, and he moved to the edge of the pool. A few moments later he cried out, "It's a raven! He's flying high over the fields and trees. He's beautiful!"

"It's my turn!" Blaise exclaimed as he pushed his way to the edge of the pool and began bouncing on the balls of his feet in excited expectation. "Come on alligator, come on tiger, come on black bear!" he chanted. But soon

The Charm Tree

enough, Blaise dropped his arms in disappointment and announced in mournful disbelief, "There's nothing. How come I don't get one?"

"Why don't you look closer?" Nerrivik prompted.

Suddenly, Blaise noticed a small, black and white head that popped out momentarily over the edge of the pool before drawing back quickly.

"What the—?" Blaise uttered, perplexed.

The creature's head reemerged, and Blaise cried out in a horribly dejected voice, "A *raccoon*?"

"Never underestimate the power of the animal which shows itself to you," Nerrivik explained patiently. "Some of the greatest qualities come from the smallest of creatures."

A disturbing thought suddenly occurred to Megan. "If we can see things in the pool, can the pool see out?" she asked in a concerned voice.

Nerrivik gave Megan a searching look. "Sometimes," she answered. "But as long as you do no wrong within the circle of the Tree, you should have nothing to worry about."

Megan lowered her eyes and pretended to concern herself with her boots. Presently, Sharindra entered the clearing and approached them eagerly. She greeted Nerrivik warmly.

"Nerrivik, you haven't come to the Harvesting in ages. What a special treat to have you here."

"I suddenly had the urge to come this year," Nerrivik explained.

As Sharindra led the group out of the clearing and towards the palace, with Dwindle following close behind, Megan looked up at Nerrivik nervously. Could she have seen what Megan had done? Megan tried to push the thought from her mind.

The children passed the rest of the day happily with their new Wynterwynian friends. Megan had told the others what Sharindra had explained to her about the stone statues, and they were amazed. Megan laughed as Winkler tackled Blaise and held him down while Stinkler built a tiny snowman on top of his head in retaliation for Blaise's actions back in Shansymoon. Even Kharn joined in the fun and lifted the children high up onto the ice sculptures.

As Megan looked at the trees, she became more and more certain that they *were* moving as she had suspected on her first evening in Wynterwyn. Long branches swayed subtly like limbs, and sometimes, Megan thought she could discern faces in the bark or evergreen needles. *Spirits of the trees*, Megan told herself and smiled.

The Charm Tree

Megan began to love the enchanted valley and thought that she could stay in Wynterwyn forever, but her thoughts kept returning to the charm under her pillow. Megan felt that she had an important job to do back home, and she couldn't let herself forget it.

Soon, everyone was called into the palace for the beginning of the festivities. The children were amazed when they entered the large hall. Sparkling lights hung from the high ceiling, and festive garlands fringed every table. The purple torches on the walls were supplemented with candles burning a soft, rose-coloured flame on all of the tables, which were arranged in a square around the crystal fountain. Fairies fluttering around the ceiling dropped their sparkling dust everywhere, while a band of Cheswicks played strange tunes on flutes, drums and strings.

"Hey! That's my flute!" Shamus yelled out at one of the members of the band, who immediately disappeared under a table. Moments later, Megan laughed as she saw the Cheswick climbing a decorated, crystal column at the other end of the hall.

Sharindra entered the hall wearing a lovely gown of gold silk, and she was followed closely by Varian, who was dressed in a black, velvet tunic. Jared and Blaise took their toques off awkwardly as Sharindra approached.

"Children, won't you sit with us at the head table?" Sharindra asked. "The places have already been set for you."

The children followed Sharindra and Varian to the largest table, where Fardymor and Roarke were already seated. The two men hastily got up as Sharindra and Varian sat down. Megan noticed with slight amusement that, though Roarke was wearing the same gold breastplate adorned with the red dragon that he had arrived in, he had apparently attempted, rather unsuccessfully, to tame his unruly, orange hair. Fardymor wore a magnificent jacket of sky blue velvet.

Once again, the two men stood up, followed by Jared and Blaise—who looked momentarily confused by the gesture—as Nerrivik approached, dressed in an elegant gown of grey satin, and took her seat at the head table. Megan noticed that the hall was filling up quickly. Cheswicks, Fairies and even a few Warfles were making their way into the hall. Some of them joined the head table. Megan was delighted to see Kharn sit down on a huge, intricately carved wooden bench, which was undoubtedly made especially for the Warfles.

"What's this?" Blaise asked as he picked up a tiny chair from the table and inspected it. Instantly, Dwindle swooped down and, with an agitated spray of gold dust, snatched the chair from Blaise and returned it to a small,

The Charm Tree

round table, where several Fairies were now seating themselves. Tiny cups and dishes had been set on the table carefully. Megan noticed that Trix was nowhere to be seen.

Once everyone had been seated, Sharindra stood up, and everyone became silent.

"I would like to sincerely thank all of you for joining us in celebrating the Harvesting of the Charm Tree." At this, everyone began cheering and pounding on the tables. Sharindra smiled and gestured for them to be silent again.

She continued, "I believe that it is vital for the people from our world to maintain peaceful contact with humans and to give what assistance we can, for it is in the kindness of humans that we may need to turn to one day." Sharindra bowed graciously to the children. Megan found she couldn't look Sharindra in the eye.

"But first and without further ado, I bid you all a fond welcome to our marvelous feast. Enjoy!"

"Enjoy!" Stinkler repeated stupidly. Everyone laughed and cheered again as countless platters, tureens and jugs were brought out. Fiona served the head table and started ladling out steaming, orange soup. "It's called fire cracker soup," she explained to Megan. Megan tried a spoonful and started coughing immediately. "Spicy, isn't it, dear? Here, have some shimmering cider to wash it down."

Megan thought it was a wonderful feast. After her soup, she tried some pixie potpie (after being assured it wasn't made from real pixies) and then munched on some sugarplums. Water sprites danced and played gracefully within the colourful waters of the crystal fountain, and a group of Cheswick jesters came out and entertained the guests with some amazing and humorous acrobatics. Next, some Fairies—Dwindle among them—mesmerized the crowd with an enchanting dance in the air.

"Hey, if we're all in here, who's guarding the Charm Tree?" Jared asked. Megan hadn't considered it.

It was Sharindra who answered. "Wynterwyn is protected by more than just armed Cheswicks," she explained, and as Winkler turned to her abruptly from his table nearby with a wounded expression, she added hastily, "though I don't know how we could possibly get along without them." Winkler smiled contentedly and returned to his periwinkle pudding.

Sharindra continued, "My brother Varian and I have placed enchantments around Wynterwyn. No one with an evil intention towards the Tree could possibly enter into the valley. But just in case, we like to keep a close watch."

Megan looked towards Varian's seat, but she found it empty.

The Charm Tree

The Fairies had finished their delightful performance, and everyone wiped the sparkling dust out of their dreamy eyes. Fardymor stood up and moved to the center of the hall, and everyone quieted down. With a clear and strong voice he spoke aloud, "It is my great pleasure to share with you all the tale of the beginning of the Charm Tree. May it open your hearts to the great love and magic which the Tree offers to the universe." Then Fardymor opened a large scroll and began to read:

And there it was—a tiny thing
Brought forth upon a wintry wind
Down it fell towards ice and snow
In darkness deep, it sat alone

Though small it was, it had such love
For all below and all above
"Please," it said, "I've much to give"
"Please," it said, "I need to live"

A light grew strong within its core
An arm branched out, through ice it tore
Towards the sky, it fought to grow
Roots dug deep in the earth below

Heather Ray Bax

It felt such pain, caught in the fray
In frozen earth t'was doomed to stay
The bitter wind whipped 'round its boughs
Thus it stood through endless hours

Though ages passed, the Tree stood strong
It waited; it listened; it sadly longed
"They're coming," the winds whispered at long last
"It's time to heal a land so vast"

A tremor ran throughout its limbs
The time had come for wondrous things!
A love grown strong through all the years
Burst forth in a shower of glistening tears

The wintry wind blew an icy blast
It stayed the tears and held them fast
The light within the Tree shone bright
Many hues pierced the endless night

Others witnessed the sky aflame
Over the mountains, many came
Within a vale they found the Tree
Those standing 'round fell to their knees

The Charm Tree

The Tree looked upon the gathered crowd
This enchanted night, it spoke aloud:
"Take my tears to those in need
Make haste with Fairy's winged speed!"

Those gathered 'round clasped hands and sang
Towards the sky, their voices rang
"These gifts will keep the babes from harm
Oh blessed be the Tree of Charms!"

Fardymor's words were greeted with a solemn silence. Megan felt a deep sadness within her; she had no idea the spirit of the Tree had endured so much to help her people. She thought that she could almost feel the pain within the Tree at that very moment…

All of a sudden, there was a loud bang on the palace doors, and shouting could be heard from outside in the grounds. Shamus jumped up to open the doors, but they wouldn't open. Roarke went over to help, but to no avail. Apparently, someone had barricaded the doors from the outside.

"What's going on?" Helena asked.

Sharindra jumped up and screamed, "The Tree is in danger—we have to get to the clearing *now*!"

Amid the sudden chaos of scrambling Cheswicks, shrieking Fairies and stomping Warfles, Roarke grabbed one of the large wooden benches, and he and Kharn used it as a battering ram to attempt to knock the doors down. Some Cheswicks tried to break the windows with chairs, but they held fast.

Sharindra moved closer to the doors as she spoke words in a language that the children couldn't understand. At once, the doors began to glow with a strange, blue light. Moments later, Roarke and Kharn succeeded in breaking the palace doors open.

With Sharindra in the lead, everyone ran out into the cold, wintry night. The Warfles that had been out in the grounds were tied up and lying in the snow. Several people ran over to help them. Megan was dismayed to see that many of the Warfles' precious ice sculptures had been destroyed. She heard the frightened baying of the stags, and her heart leapt into her throat.

When Sharindra had reached the circular clearing, with the others following close behind, she stopped short and fell to her knees. There, before her, was the Charm Tree, lying on its side with its roots completely torn from the earth. Not a single glimmer of light was to be seen from its delicate branches.

★ 13 ★
The Light Grows Dim

The sight of the Charm Tree in such disgrace horrified Megan. The bright moonlight revealed tracks around the Tree that suggested many had been here. Megan's heart sank as she noticed some tracks that were ten times the size of the others—even Warfles had helped. Dwindle and the other Fairies flew to the Tree and threw themselves, weeping, onto its lifeless limbs and hollow charms. Sharindra let her head fall as tears began to stream down her face.

Fardymor attempted to comfort her, but Sharindra cried out with despair, "*I* was the appointed Guardian—*I* failed the Tree!"

Megan felt a cold chill and wrapped her arms around herself.

"The Tree is still here; can't we replant it?" Helena suggested hopefully.

It was Nerrivik who answered, "Even though it was uprooted, the Tree, along with its charms, could still have had life left in it. It must have been an evil spell which took its light."

Despite her pain at seeing the Charm Tree destroyed, Megan looked back at her bedroom window in the palace hopefully. *Maybe her charm was still all right.*

Roarke crashed his large fist down angrily onto a nearby hitching rail, causing the stags to snort and fidget nervously. "No one with an evil intention towards the Tree could have gotten into Wynterwyn! The enchantments wouldn't have allowed it!" he stated firmly.

"They could if they had been helped by someone who was already *in* Wynterwyn—someone who had the power to weaken the protective enchantments," Sharindra replied flatly.

"Varian," Fardymor breathed.

Sharindra looked at the Charm Tree with utter despair. "I didn't see this coming. I couldn't see the darkness in my own brother."

Nerrivik looked down at Sharindra warmly. "You didn't *want* to see it in your brother, Sharindra. None of us did."

The Charm Tree

Nerrivik glanced in Megan's direction before adding, "If we had even one glowing charm left, we could replant it in this soil where the Charm Tree has stood so bravely for ages upon ages. Then we might have a chance of bringing the light back to Wynterwyn."

Megan felt her face flush, and she began to feel very uneasy. She *couldn't* give her charm back! What if they planted it and it didn't work—what if the Tree didn't grow back? The charm would be lost. What would become of her little brother then?

"There is no light left in the charms," Sharindra uttered as she stood up.

A cold wind began to pick up as Blaise screamed out, "There must be something we can do!"

"There's nothing," Sharindra replied dejectedly. "The evil ones have succeeded."

Sharindra turned to leave the clearing, and others followed. Soon, only the children and Nerrivik remained. Snow began to fall around them as Nerrivik continued to watch Megan intently. Megan became frightened, and she turned to leave the clearing.

"I know you have a charm, Megan," Nerrivik stated. Megan whipped around. Her friends turned to look at her with confused expressions.

"In my pool—I saw you take it while the others were at the race. The charms belong to humans, and therefore,

I cannot take it from you. But you have to give it back, Megan; it's the only way to save the Charm Tree. It's the only way to save your own people!"

Megan turned to her friends. She didn't like the way they were looking at her. It made her feel like they were silently accusing *her* of killing the Tree. Megan felt dark anger and resentment rising within her.

"I took it for Nicky! It's mine, and I won't give it back!" she cried before turning and running from the clearing. Megan raced back to the palace and up to her room. She grabbed the glowing charm from under her pillow and pushed it into her coat pocket. Then Megan raced back outside and through the chaotic palace grounds, desperate to find the flower ring and go back to her world.

A cold wind bit her face mercilessly as Megan passed by the broken ice sculptures and Shamus and Fiona's tree house. When she reached the place where she guessed she and the other children had veered off the path on their first evening in Wynterwyn, she turned and plunged frantically into the trees. Megan stopped short. There, before her, was the enchanted, purple tulip within its glowing ring of crystals. All Megan had to do was step into the circle, and she would be back with Mr. White Bear, safe and sound.

Megan fell to her knees and pulled the charm out of her pocket. It still shone out with its ethereal, green

The Charm Tree

light, but Megan noticed with dismay that the charm had already lost some of its brilliance. Megan closed her eyes. She could feel the spirit of the Charm Tree calling to her on the wind. Could she take the charm back to her brother, knowing that all of the other babies in her world would suffer? Megan sighed and felt a tear slide down her cheek; she knew she couldn't.

Megan stood up and began to make her way back towards the palace slowly. No one was in sight. Apparently, everyone had returned to their homes, believing that there was nothing that could be done and wanting to escape from the cold, blustery night. Megan looked upon the deserted grounds, the broken palace doors and the damaged ice sculptures. *There* was *something she could do!* Megan told herself firmly.

Megan began to run against the driving snow and biting wind until she had reached the circular clearing. Once there, she stood beside the gaping hole where the Charm Tree had been ripped from the earth and she held the charm over it. Megan knew all she had to do was drop the charm in and cover it with snow. She had made her decision, and she smiled, knowing that it was the right thing to do.

Megan heard a voice from behind her, and she whipped around. Varian emerged from the shadows of the trees surrounding the clearing, the wind blowing his hair and long, black cape. He was carrying a large, empty vial in one hand and what appeared to be a wand with a glowing, red stone on its tip in the other. Megan felt a wave of anger run through her. Apparently, Varian had remained to make sure his evil work had proceeded according to plan.

"What a fortunate meeting this is," Varian said, smiling acidly. "I always knew that humans were not to be trusted. I saw you and your friends entering Wynterwyn, and I tried to get rid of you quickly with a flower ring, but that disgusting dog pulled you back. However, it would appear that even *I* underestimated your potential for betrayal. I didn't count on you stealing a charm from the *beloved* Tree. You could have ruined everything that I worked so hard to achieve."

Megan felt her anger growing hot within her. "You shouldn't be talking about betrayal, Varian! You broke your sister's heart when she realized what you had done."

Varian laughed bitterly. "What broke my sister's heart was knowing that she didn't have her precious position as Guardian of the Charm Tree anymore. No one will praise her or show her honour now—now that she has *failed!*" Varian spat. Suddenly, Megan saw Varian for what he truly was.

"You didn't do this terrible thing out of hatred for humans! You did this out of jealousy for your sister!"

The Charm Tree

"Enough of this!" Varian cried with wild eyes. "Give me the charm *now!*"

Megan flinched at the ferocity of Varian's demand, and she dropped the charm into the snow beside her. As she bent down quickly to pick it up, Varian raised his wand and started speaking strange words. Megan cried out as she felt an intense coldness, like ice, flowing swiftly through her limbs. Within moments, Megan was completely immobilized—frozen like one of Kharn's ice sculptures.

Varian slowly walked over to Megan and snatched the charm from her frozen hand. "Humans only know how to steal and destroy," he whispered into Megan's ear. "They cut down forests and pollute the land and waters, harming the beings of nature without a second thought. The actions of humans affect the whole universe. Now they'll know what it feels like to have something *they* treasure destroyed." Varian sank back into the darkness of the trees, leaving Megan with no choice but to ponder his words.

It took several minutes for Varian's freezing spell to wear off. Megan knew she wouldn't be able to catch up to him now, and even if she could, she knew she was no match against Varian's magic alone. Megan ran back to the palace. The great hall was deserted, so Megan ran to the room she shared with Helena. There she found Helena, Blaise and Jared.

"I tried to replant the charm!" Megan gushed when she saw her friends. "I tried, but Varian came back and took it from me!"

"Don't even try to convince us of that!" Helena spat. "I saw you running towards the forest. You were heading for the flower ring."

"You could have gone back home already and hidden your precious charm before catching a ride back here on a magic daisy," Blaise added, frowning.

"I did go back to the flower ring," Megan cried desperately, "but I found I couldn't do it—I couldn't take the charm back to Nicky. Don't you see, I knew it was all wrong!"

"We can't trust anything you say anymore," Helena said as she turned away from Megan. Megan turned to Jared and looked at him pleadingly. Megan thought she saw sympathy in his eyes, but her hope faded when his eyes slowly moved to the floor.

Megan left the room dejectedly and went back to the hall. The empty tables in the festive room was a sad sight. Megan didn't know what to do. If her best friends wouldn't believe the truth, no one would.

The Charm Tree

Suddenly, Stinkler popped his head in through the palace doors, with Winkler's head appearing just above his a moment later.

"We saw, we saw!" Stinkler said, grinning.

"The charm!" Winkler added.

"You saw what happened?" Megan asked.

Both of the Cheswick brothers nodded vigorously as Kharn's huge body appeared behind them in the doorway. As the Warfle bent down to look in, Dwindle landed down on Winkler's shoulder with a flutter of her wings. A moment later, Jack appeared. He let out a solitary bark as a greeting.

"We know what you tried to do," Dwindle said in her delicate, high-pitched voice.

Megan ran to them. "Will you help me get the charm back?" she asked hopefully.

"Yes, yes!" Stinkler replied.

"Steal it back!" Winkler added cheerfully.

Megan was so grateful. Even after she had stolen one of their precious treasures, the Wynterwynians were still willing to help her. "We'll have to leave now," Megan said. "The charm is quickly losing its light, and Varian will certainly perform a spell on it once he gets a safe distance from the palace."

"Jack can find his tracks," Dwindle said.

So they all went out into the storm and made their way towards the clearing. Megan couldn't bear to look at the Charm Tree as Jack turned and led them into the forest.

They had to move quickly to catch up with Varian. Winkler and Stinkler were able to follow Jack quite deftly through the trees. Though they were very close, Megan had to look hard to see them in the dark. Dwindle dimmed her light and kept to the tree branches, where she blended in nicely with the blowing tree limbs. Even Kharn, who was so big, moved quickly through the forest without making a sound. Megan found it difficult to keep up, and the cold wind was whipping snow around her furiously. Kharn stopped and picked her up, placing her gently on top of his shoulders. Megan was grateful for the rest and the warmth of his thick, white fur.

After they had traveled quite a distance, Jack stopped suddenly. Megan looked up and could see smoke rising from the treetops just ahead. Kharn set her down and they all crept closer for a better look. There was Varian, standing in a small clearing near a blazing fire, stirring a steaming substance in a big, black pot. With the wind whipping his hair wildly about his face and his dark cape blowing behind him, Megan thought Varian looked like a true sorcerer.

The Charm Tree

A few Cheswicks were keeping guard around the clearing, while others were dancing around merrily. Some Warfles were sitting in the snow, and Fairies zipped around the fire, giggling and letting their sparkling dust fall in their excitement. But Megan noticed with horror that many of these creatures looked different from the Wynterwynians. Just as Sharindra had explained, hatred had turned them into ugly and fierce-looking monsters.

Megan scowled when she spotted Trix standing on Varian's shoulder triumphantly. Dwindle noticed her as well, and she momentarily let her gold light shine brightly in her anger. Kharn quickly stepped in front of her to avoid having her seen.

"Stop this!" Varian screamed at the others. "You know I have to concentrate. I used up all of the potion on that wretched tree, and now I have to make more to kill this charm." Varian gestured to the charm, which was lying on a broken tree stump. "It's losing its light quickly, but if there's even a glimmer left within it, and they get it back, all of our plans will be destroyed."

Megan looked at the charm, and a thought suddenly occurred to her. She pulled out the charm that her father had given her. If Megan could switch the charms without Varian seeing, they could sneak back to the clearing and plant the glowing charm without Varian and his people being the wiser. But they didn't have much time; Megan needed a distraction. She huddled with the others, and soon they had hatched a plan.

Winkler and Stinkler would sneak around to the other side of the clearing, while Kharn would go to the right and Jack to the left. Dwindle would stay with Megan, and once the Fairy had given the signal—by letting herself shine brightly—the others would make loud noises and attract the attention of Varian's people. While the others were being chased through the trees, Megan would sneak into the clearing and switch the charms. Then she would run back to the palace with the others doubling back to join her.

The others agreed, and Megan sent them off. When Megan felt that they must have reached their places, she turned to Dwindle and nodded once. For a brief moment, Dwindle let herself shine out. Immediately, Jack started barking loudly, Winkler and Stinkler yelled out nasty taunts and Kharn began making such a racket that even Megan thought the whole forest must be crashing down.

Instantly, the Cheswicks in the clearing stopped dancing. The Fairies hovered in midair, while the Warfles stood up and looked from side to side stupidly, obviously perplexed.

"Don't just stand there!" Varian screamed at them. "Go and find them!"

The Charm Tree

As Varian's people crashed into the trees, Megan could hear Jack's barking and the Cheswick's taunts getting farther and farther away. She hoped they would all get back to the palace safely. Now there was only Varian and Trix left in the clearing. Megan watched as Varian left his potion and walked to the far side of the clearing to peer out into the darkness; Trix remained on his shoulder.

It's now or never, Megan told herself. With her heart beating wildly, Megan crept into the clearing and made her way towards the tree stump. Once there, she took her charm off of its chain and placed it on the stump. With the fierce wind whipping her hair around her face, Megan grabbed the other charm, which now only contained the faintest glimmer of light, and put it into her coat pocket. Megan turned back and was almost to the edge of the clearing when Trix suddenly screamed out, "It's the girl! She's getting away!"

Megan felt as though her heart had stopped. A mere moment later, she perceived Dwindle swooping over her head as she dived towards Trix. Megan turned back to see the two Fairies struggling in midair with gold and purple dust shooting out all around them. Varian was staring at Megan with a look of pure hatred in his eyes as he took his wand from his robes and slowly raised it. Megan fell down into the snow as tears began to fill her eyes. She felt that it was all over.

"Humans have always been weak!" Varian spat. "Look at you—kneeling in the snow and crying. You have nothing to offer the universe but weakness and destruction."

At once, Megan felt intense anger flowing through her. She looked at Varian, and she saw the faces of all of the people who had ever belittled her and made her feel less than what she was. Megan stood up straight and held her arms out against the icy blasts of the storm, the wind blowing her open jacket out like wings, and she faced Varian with her head held high. "You're wrong!" she screamed. "I am Megan Whittlebee from Shansymoon Creek, and I have more to offer the universe than an evil sorcerer like you could ever dream of!"

Shock flashed across Varian's face momentarily. It was replaced quickly with red hot lightning, however, as Varian raised his wand towards Megan and opened his mouth to utter a spell.

Not this time! Megan thought. She whipped around and lunged into the shadows of the trees, falling face-first into the cold snow. Instantly, she was up again, and with a last concerned glance towards Dwindle, Megan began to race back in the direction of the palace. She could hear Varian's enraged screams close behind her. Despite the cold wind and freezing snow that bit her face savagely, Megan didn't slow down. She knew it was imperative that she get back to the palace and replant the charm as soon as possible or all would be lost.

With her heart beating madly in her chest, Megan glanced around fearfully. Was she going in the right direction? Suddenly, Megan's breath caught in her throat as she felt something grab her leg and pull her down into darkness. A cold hand reached out to cover Megan's mouth so that she couldn't scream out.

★ 14 ★
Megan's Light Shines

"Megan," a voice whispered. Megan nearly fainted with relief as she recognized the voice as belonging to her cousin Blaise.

Megan heard Helena's voice too. "We changed our minds and wanted to help you, and we ran into Winkler and Stinkler in the clearing. They brought us here to their tunnels and showed us a shortcut to where you were."

"Shortcut tunnels!" Stinkler repeated enthusiastically.

"Shh!" the others said.

Megan's eyes began to adjust to the darkness of the tunnel they were in. "Thanks, guys. I'm so glad you're here," she whispered as gratitude for her friends flooded through her. "Varian was right on my tail. We need to get to the clearing and replant the charm as soon as possible."

"Right, that means you two are in the lead," Jared said to Winkler and Stinkler.

In a flash, the two Cheswick brothers were up and running down the tunnel. It was a challenge for the children to keep up without tripping over the various items that were strewn about the rough, dirt floor. A few torches burned here and there, providing the only light in the vast labyrinth of tunnels.

As they were passing through a wider section of tunnel, they came across a Cheswick child sitting atop a large, dirty pile of clothes, broken dishes and damp books. The child appeared entranced with an object that was glowing with a greenish light and emitting a strange sort of music. It was a video game console.

"Hey, that's mine!" Jared cried as he reached his hand out and snatched the device from the tiny Cheswick, who immediately stood up on his pile like he was a king and stuck out his tongue with indignation.

The children continued to follow Winkler and Stinkler, and Cheswicks began to poke their heads out of small rooms and adjoining tunnels. A group of curious followers started to form, following the children through the tunnels like they were in a procession.

The Charm Tree

"Parade!" One Cheswick suddenly cried out and banged on a pair of tattered cymbals.

"No, don't do that!" Megan whispered desperately. "We don't want to be discovered."

Winkler stepped out in front and informed the other Cheswicks to go away with a superior wave of his arm. With scornful faces, the congregated group slinked back into the shadows of the tunnels.

"This way," Stinkler said and pointed to a small, dark tunnel. "Charm Tree."

Megan led the way into the tunnel and soon saw a patch of bright moonlight. Warily, she crept out of the tunnel and into the fierce storm. The others followed close behind.

Megan spotted the circular clearing. "Follow me," she whispered, and the children made their way quickly into the clearing. The cold wind whipped furiously, and the white stags bayed and pawed at the ground anxiously as Megan took the charm out of her pocket and held it up. With dismay, Megan noticed that there was only a flicker of green light left in its core. Megan moved towards the gaping hole where the magnificent Charm Tree had once stood, and she was stopped in her tracks. Varian walked out from behind the felled Tree, holding his wand high.

"You're too late!" he cried out triumphantly. "The light has almost gone out in the charm, and if you make one move towards that hole, I will give you a freezing that will never unthaw!"

Jared looked from Varian to the charm in Megan's hand. Then he shot his twin sister a meaningful look. Helena nodded her understanding, while Blaise stood by, looking obviously puzzled.

Suddenly, Jared lunged towards Varian, who pointed his wand at him and began to speak the words that would freeze him. Megan cried out with despair as Jared halted instantly and began to seize up. A shell of ice was forming around his body.

While Varian was still concentrating on Jared, Helena shouted, "Now, Blaise!" and she and Blaise pounced on Varian, causing him to fall back into the snow.

"Plant the charm now!" Helena cried out to Megan as Blaise wrestled the wand from Varian's hand.

Megan fell to her knees and dropped the charm into the hole. With a wild fury she began scooping up snow and throwing it onto the charm.

"No!" she heard Varian cry out as Helena and Blaise constrained him.

There was a loud sound of something crashing through the forest. Megan turned to see Varian's people entering the clearing. When they saw their master struggling in the snow, they pulled Helena and Blaise off of him savagely and restrained them. Varian stood up and brushed the

The Charm Tree

snow off of his cape angrily as Trix alighted upon his shoulder.

"You're the one who is too late, Varian!" Megan screamed at him. "The charm is planted! You've lost!"

Varian looked over to the spot where Megan had planted the charm with fear in his eyes. For several moments he stared. Then, to Megan's surprise, Varian threw his head back and began to laugh. The sinister sound sent chills down Megan's spine.

"It didn't work!" Varian cried out viciously. "The charm had lost all of its light before you planted it; otherwise, we would be witnessing a tree growing before us even as we speak."

Megan's heart sank as she too looked at the snow where she had planted the charm. *Could it be true?* It *was* true. Not a single movement or flicker of light could be seen from the spot.

Varian retrieved his wand and spoke the words that would freeze Helena and Blaise. Then he turned back to Megan and sneered. "Now you're all alone with no one left to protect you."

Megan began to perceive a white form appearing in the pool behind Varian. It took the shape of a swan, which spread out its wings and held its graceful head high.

"I'm never alone," Megan replied calmly.

All of a sudden, there were voices and barking from the direction of the palace. Jack came trotting into the clearing, followed by Sharindra, Fardymor, Nerrivik and Roarke. As the clearing began to fill with Wynterwynians, Kharn, Dwindle and the Cheswick brothers emerged from the trees behind Varian's people.

Varian appeared unnerved for a moment before regaining his cool composure. It was Sharindra who spoke first.

"What has happened here?" she demanded as she took in Varian's wand and the frozen forms of the children.

It was Megan who answered. "I stole a charm from the Charm Tree, Sharindra. I was going to take it back to my baby brother Nicholas, who is very sick. When the Tree was destroyed, I tried to escape Wynterwyn with the charm, but I couldn't do it. I knew it was wrong. When I tried to replant the charm, Varian took it from me."

Kharn, Dwindle, Jack and the Cheswick brothers came nearer and stood around Megan. Megan continued, "My friends and I went to get the charm back, and it has been replanted.

Sharindra looked from Megan to the place where the Tree had stood. "The light within the charm has died," she said sadly.

The Charm Tree

"That's right, Sharindra," Varian said bitterly. "The Tree is dead and can never come back. Without it, the race of humans will not last long."

Megan's heart plummeted. She felt that she had failed and that it was her fault the Charm Tree was gone forever. Megan felt Jack's wet nose on the back of her hand. She looked down and saw the charm that her father had given her in his mouth; Jack had gone back for it. Megan was touched. She took it gratefully and held it in her hand.

Megan felt a warm surge of love flow through her—love for her brother, love for her friends, who had risked much to help her, and love for all of the humans who would suffer without the Charm Tree. She wished deep in her heart that she could do something to save the Tree for the people of her world.

At once, bright beams of light began to shoot out from between the fingers of Megan's tightly clutched hand. Shocked, she opened her hand to reveal the charm—warm and glowing with a vibrant, pink light within its core.

"What's happening?" Megan asked. "I thought the light in this charm had gone out long ago."

Fardymor came over and placed his hand on Megan's shoulder. "This is the charm of extraordinary love, Megan. It's the same gift that you had received as a baby. It was your love which brought the light back within it."

"But how did I do this?" Megan asked, perplexed.

This time it was Nerrivik who spoke. "Megan Whittlebee, you carry a light within you, which no one else can carry. Without you, the universe would be incomplete. Without you, the Tree cannot be saved."

Varian was horrified. "No!" he screamed. "This can't be!"

All eyes were on Megan as she carried the charm to the center of the clearing and placed it in the snow carefully. Dwindle and the Fairies flew down to watch as Megan placed snow on top of the glowing charm. Almost instantly, the cold wind died down, and large snowflakes began to fall gently. Pink light shone out from the snow, and a tremor could be felt within the ground. Megan stood back and watched as a silver branch pushed its way through the snow tentatively. It grew larger and began to shoot out other branches. Small charms began to grow on the branches, and their bright light shone out in every direction. Soon, the children and Wynterwynians were gathered around a wondrous new Charm Tree, and they were silent with awe.

A soft breeze blew through the clearing, and Megan could feel the hairs standing up on the back of her neck as though there was charged energy all around her, hugging her. She heard a beautiful voice whisper, "Thank you," before witnessing a graceful and radiant spirit descend upon the Tree. The limbs of the Tree shuddered momentarily, as

The Charm Tree

though stretching after a long and deep sleep. Megan felt joy surge through her, and tears came to her eyes.

The Wynterwynians began to cheer loudly. All of the Fairies flew to the Tree and began to dance merrily on its bright branches as Jared, Helena and Blaise began to come out of their freezing.

Varian cried out in horror before he and his people fled back into the inky shadows of the forest.

Megan walked over to her friends. "We're really sorry we didn't believe you, Meg," Blaise said awkwardly as he stuffed his hands deep into his pockets and looked down at his shuffling feet.

"I wish we had been there to help you get the charm back," Jared added. Helena nodded her agreement.

Megan smiled at her friends. "It's all right," she said. "I'm not sure if I would have believed me either. It means a lot to me that you changed your mind and came after me."

After hugs and more than a few tears, the children joined the Wynterwynians in celebrating the return of the Charm Tree. Soon, however, it was time for the Fairies to depart. Fardymor stood forward and spoke aloud:

> Dear Fairies with your shining grace
> Pluck a charm and hold it safe
> Up towards the stars, take flight

> Upon this most enchanted night
> To the babes, fly fast and free
> Upon this wind I raise for thee

The children watched Fardymor with amazement as he uttered strange words and conjured a soft, warm wind. Soon, countless Fairies were entering the clearing from every direction in a loud chorus of whispering and beating wings. Each one took a charm from the Tree before taking off on the enchanted wind into the starry, night sky. Megan's thoughts flew to Nicholas as she wondered which charm he would receive. She smiled knowing that he would receive the gift he was meant to have.

The next day saw another grand feast in honour of Megan and her friends. Seated at the head table with the children were the Cheswick brothers and Dwindle, who had returned with the other Fairies early that morning. Kharn's large, wooden bench had also been pulled up to the table, and he shared it with Jack, who eagerly ate his meal from a shiny, gold dish.

Once everyone had finished eating, Sharindra stood up and made a toast. "Today we honour our dear friend Megan Whittlebee, who risked and sacrificed much to bring the Charm Tree back to us. Without her, the Tree

The Charm Tree

would certainly have been lost for all time. It is my belief that Megan's great deed will be told and retold among our people throughout all of the ages."

In response, all of the Wynterwynians stood and cheered. Helena also stood up and cheered loudly, while Blaise and Jared pounded on the table, shouting, "Let's go Megan, let's go!" Megan felt her face flush, but she didn't hide herself away. Instead, she grabbed her goblet of shimmering cider and toasted Blaise and the twins as well as her new friends from Wynterwyn for helping her. Everyone cheered once more.

Megan sat back down and turned to Sharindra. "What will become of Varian and his people?" she asked.

Sharindra looked at her brother's empty chair regretfully. "Varian and the others have fled from Wynterwyn. The enchantments that surround our valley have been strengthened and will never allow them to return." Sharindra turned to Megan and smiled. "Because of you the Charm Tree will always remain safe."

Megan smiled back.

Suddenly, Winkler jumped up onto the table and did a head stand, while Stinkler yelled, "Presents!" The Cheswicks darted under the table and soon reemerged with an odd assortment of things. Helena found her pink ballet slippers and amber ring falling into her lap, while

Fiona was presented with her bumbleberry teapot. Jared's video game console flew over and hit him in the chest.

"Hey, I had already taken this back!" he said, perplexed.

Shamus pulled his flute out of his shirt pocket, and Blaise's Math textbook fell into his goblin goulash.

"Oh—this isn't mine," he said quickly as he threw the large book back to Stinkler.

The next thing everyone knew, Winkler had raced from the room and reentered leading the baby green dragon. He took it over to Roarke and said sheepishly, "Wouldn't fit in Winkler's tunnel."

The hall rang out with laughter as shimmering cider filled every goblet, and an endless parade of dessert platters were brought out from the kitchen.

"Hey, do you realize that we've been in Wynterwyn for four days?" Jared asked the others. "It's Christmas back home!" The children looked at one another with surprise. Megan remembered her parents with guilt. She had promised them that she would be home by now. The children decided regretfully that it was time to go home.

As they walked out into the moonlit grounds, their new friends accompanied them. The children found it difficult to say goodbye. Dwindle stood daintily on Kharn's strong shoulder, while Winkler and Stinkler were still trying to give Blaise his Math textbook (who was refusing it just as insistently!). Jack sat in the snow, thumping his tail, and Shamus and Fiona stood behind him. Nerrivik stood by serenely, while Roarke attempted to control the baby green dragon.

Megan heard the faint sound of bells chiming, and she turned to see Fardymor leading Kanter towards her. Megan stroked Kanter's nose gently as she whispered, "Thanks for taking me to the stars." Kanter nuzzled her cheek in response. Megan looked up at Fardymor, and she saw his pale, blue eyes sparkle.

"I guess the charm was delivered to its rightful place after all," he said. Megan smiled broadly and threw her arms around Fardymor.

Sharindra stepped forward and gestured her hand toward the sparkling snow, where an iridescent rose appeared instantly, surrounded by glowing crystals.

"There is no need for goodbyes," she said softly. "There are many doorways into our world, and if you truly desire it, you will find one again someday. You will always be welcome in Wynterwyn."

The children looked at one another happily.

"And all of you are welcome in our world anytime," Blaise replied as he patted the green dragon on its steaming snout. "Our house is kind of full right now, but I can clean out the garage for you."

Sharindra chuckled. "Thank you for your kind invitation, Blaise."

Suddenly, Megan thought of something. She turned to Shamus and Fiona. "Are you sure you won't come back with us?" she asked.

"Oh no, dear," Fiona said. "Wynterwyn is our home now; we couldn't imagine ourselves anywhere else." Jack barked his agreement.

As the children stepped, one by one, into the flower ring, they thought of home and of how much they missed their families. Megan thought of Nicholas, and sadness crept into her heart. She wondered if he was safe and home from the hospital.

★ 15 ★
Home

The children found themselves standing in the snow at the base of a steep hill and blinking into the last of the late afternoon sun. When they turned around, they saw the mouth of the ice tunnel they had slid into several days earlier.

"We're back home!" Jared declared. "All we need to do is climb back up this hill and walk east towards Grandpa's house."

The children heard a voice calling out.

"It's Grandpa!" Helena said happily before calling back.

"Let's hurry," Megan suggested, and the children started up the steep hill. It was an arduous climb, and the children were panting once they had reached the top.

Within moments, they saw the large figure of Mr. White Bear rushing towards them.

"Children, what are you doing way over here? You shouldn't be sledding on these slopes; they're too steep and dangerous."

"Grandpa, what day is it?" Helena asked excitedly, bouncing on her toes.

"What do you mean?" her grandfather asked, puzzled. "It's Saturday. The day hasn't changed since you all went out this morning to play in the snow."

The children looked at one another with awe.

"Sharindra was right," Megan said. "We came back to the same time and place from which we left."

As Mr. White Bear led the children back towards his house, they spoke all at once, gushing over Wynterwyn and all of the people they had met and the miraculous things that had happened.

"I flew a dragon, Grandpa!" Blaise said.

"My spirit animal is a raven," Jared announced proudly.

"Well, I won a race to the stars," Helena declared as she held up the gold star that Sharindra had presented to her.

"And I got third place," Megan added as she held up her blue star.

The Charm Tree

Mr. White Bear stopped to inspect Helena and Megan's stars. He looked thoughtful for a moment.

"Don't you believe us?" Jared cried.

"Of course I believe you, Jared," his grandfather replied. "Why don't you tell me more over supper; I have the chili ready, and you skipped lunch today."

The children's hearts sank. It would seem that Mr. White Bear didn't truly believe them.

Mr. White Bear gazed down at them with a twinkle in his eyes. "Then again, you've probably eaten several meals in the land you visited."

The children smiled at one another.

"I could go on and on about the food!" Blaise gushed with enthusiasm.

The children enjoyed the rest of their days with Mr. White Bear—playing in the snow, sipping hot chocolate and telling the older man all about their adventures. Too soon, Baxter came driving down the lane, and it was time for the children to say goodbye.

After Mr. White Bear had passed out wrapped presents for the children to take home with them, Jared and Helena gave their grandfather a hug. "We'll come back soon," they promised. Next, Blaise and Megan approached the older man and gave him a hug.

"Don't forget," he whispered, "you're never alone."

The children piled into the back of the black Cadillac and waved at Mr. White Bear as the car pulled away. Once the log house was out of sight, the children shot a meaningful look at one another before ripping open their presents.

Megan had received a beautiful, wooden carving of a swan that had been painted carefully with intricate detail. She was delighted to see that it had its wings spread open, and its graceful head was held high. The other children had also received carvings of their spirit animals.

"I guess a raccoon isn't so bad," Blaise declared thoughtfully. "They have faces that make them look like bandits, and they're always stealing people's junk—like Cheswicks!" Blaise proceeded to make an impersonation of Stinkler, which had the other children hooting with laughter—and plugging their noses!

When they had entered Shansymoon Creek, the children asked Baxter if they could stop at the candy shop to pick up some snacks. Once inside, Megan passed around a corner into the chocolate aisle and ran right into Lacy Reilly, causing her to drop her bag of sour pops.

"I'm sorry," Megan said as she bent down to pick up the bag.

The Charm Tree

"You idiot!" Lacy cried. "Now look what you've made me do. I ought to take you outside and bury you in the snow!"

Megan stood up and squared her shoulders. She looked into Lacy's eyes deeply and saw the true weakness and insecurity that lay behind her fury. Megan spoke in a menacing tone, "I've faced up to bigger and better than you, Lacy Reilly, and I wouldn't be at all afraid to give you a fistful of badness."

Fear suddenly came into Lacy's eyes, and she backed up, bumping into a dark-haired boy who was choosing a chocolate bar. As Megan took two steps towards her, Lacy spun on her heels and ran from the shop, forgetting all about her sour pops.

On the way to Mavilyn Mansion, Helena, Jared and Blaise gushed over Megan's scene in the candy shop.

"Baxter, you should have seen Lacy's face as she ran out the door!" Jared said, laughing.

"I thought she was going to pee her pants," Helena added with a giggle.

"Yeah, but she's still so cute," Blaise declared with a dreamy look on his face. Helena grabbed her licorice and hit him over the head with it.

Once the car had pulled up in front of Mavilyn Mansion, Mrs. Mavilyn came out to greet the children.

"Did you have a good time?" she asked.

"Did we ever!" Jared exclaimed.

Megan remembered something and looked up at the older woman.

"Mrs. Mavilyn, do you know where those statues of the elves in the theatre grounds came from?"

Mrs. Mavilyn looked down at Megan thoughtfully. "Yes, of course," she replied. "Years ago I had them commissioned based on something I had seen once as a child." The older woman's eyes lit up. "That's an interesting tale I'll have to tell you all someday."

The children looked at one another with wide eyes.

Blaise looked up anxiously at the menacing gargoyles adorning the front steps.

"You didn't have those made based on something you had seen, did you?"

"Good heavens, no," Mrs. Mavilyn replied and chuckled. "Why ever do you ask?"

Blaise let out an audible sigh of relief. "No reason," he said, trying to sound unconcerned.

"But those stone dragons above the doors at the theatre are another story," Mrs. Mavilyn added off-handedly.

Blaise choked on a caramel.

Mrs. Mavilyn looked down at Megan and Blaise and smiled. "Well, I'm sure your parents are eager to see you both. Why don't you let Baxter drive you home? I think

The Charm Tree

you'll be pleasantly surprised by what you find," she said and winked at Megan.

Megan and Blaise said their goodbyes and got back into the car. When they had pulled up in front of their house, Megan's parents opened the front door and stepped out. To Megan's delight, her father was holding Nicholas in his arms.

Megan jumped out of the car and rushed up the stairs to greet him. "I tried my best," she whispered as she kissed her little brother on the cheek. He grabbed her finger affectionately.

———◆———

That night was Christmas Eve. After Megan had put on her pajamas, she walked over to her parents' room, where Nicholas had his crib. He was still awake and playing with his green bunny. Blaise entered the room and joined Megan beside the crib.

"We're so lucky," he said. "We get two Christmases this year."

"Yeah," Megan agreed as she adjusted Nicholas's blanket. Suddenly, Megan looked up at Blaise with wide eyes; she had just realized something. "Tonight is the night the Fairies deliver the charms to the babies," she said excitedly.

Megan and Blaise ran to the window and looked out. In the distance, they saw a tiny pinprick of light that was becoming larger. Blaise threw open the window, and a tiny Fairy with silver hair and a pink dress landed on the ledge. She was carrying a glowing, gold charm that Megan recognized as the charm of music.

The Fairy looked at the children and twitched her wings before fluttering over to land on Nicholas's crib. Nicholas laughed as the Fairy tickled his cheek with her wings. Then she lightly jumped up onto his chest and placed the gold charm down, where it seemed to melt magically and disappear. The Fairy kissed Nicholas on his nose before taking off through the window and disappearing into the starry night.

Megan and Blaise looked at one another with awe. They knew they had just witnessed something very special that they would not soon forget.

On Christmas morning, Megan and Blaise woke early and ran down to the living room. Their stockings, which had been hung on the mantle of the fireplace, were overflowing with goodies, and the glowing Christmas tree was surrounded with presents. Slowly, the sleepy-eyed parents dragged themselves into the room and watched the children happily as they opened their presents. Nicholas

The Charm Tree

had more fun playing with the wrapping paper than with his new toys.

Later in the morning, there was a knock at the front door. It was Helena and Jared, and they had come bearing gifts. Blaise received a new orange toque, twice as long as his old one. Megan opened a shiny, red box to reveal a painted, clay figurine that looked just like Dwindle.

"Helena and I made it last night," Jared said.

"Jared sculpted it, and I painted it," Helena added proudly.

"It's beautiful," Megan declared and thanked her friends.

After Megan had run up to her room to place her new figurine next to her swan carving, the children went out to the theatre grounds to play. After an animated snowball fight (in which Blaise kept tripping over his trailing toque), the children fell down into the snow, laughing. Presently, the sound of a cat meowing made them turn their heads. There was Sapphire, sitting in the snow and swishing her black tail proudly as she held something in her mouth.

"What is that?" Jared asked as he moved closer for a better look. He laughed out loudly. "It's Stinkler's hat!" he cried incredulously.

The children ran to where the statues of the Cheswick brothers stood on their stone platform. Megan noticed two sets of pointed footprints that trailed off towards the theatre and back. As she looked up at Stinkler, she giggled, as she saw that—sure enough—he was missing his pointed, brown cap.

"Good going, Sapphire!" Blaise cried as the cat rubbed her body against his legs affectionately. Helena nearly fell over from the shock of seeing her cat and Blaise making friends.

That evening, Megan took Nicholas into her room and played with him on her bed. "I'm sorry I couldn't make you better," she whispered to him as a tear slid down her cheek. Megan's father entered the room and sat down on the edge of the bed.

Megan fingered the silver chain her father had given her. "Dad, there's something I have to tell you about the trinket you gave me," she said with a mischievous glint in her eye.

Megan didn't have the chance to continue, as suddenly, Nicholas's eyes widened, and he started to coo and giggle. Megan and her father turned to see what he was looking at and were astounded by what they saw. The figurine of Dwindle, which stood on Megan's bedside table, had begun to glow. Slowly, its delicate limbs began to move, and its shimmering wings twitched. Megan and her father were amazed to witness—before their very eyes—the figurine transforming into the real Dwindle. Dwindle shook herself, and gold dust flew everywhere.

Megan's father was speechless.

"What are you doing here, Dwindle?" Megan asked, hardly believing what she was seeing.

"Delivery," Dwindle replied as she held up a charm that was shining brightly with an emerald green light.

Megan was beside herself with joy as Dwindle hopped up onto her bed and carried the charm over to Nicholas.

"Grow healthy and strong, little one," Dwindle whispered as she placed the charm over Nicholas's heart, where it melted instantly and disappeared.

Dwindle flew up onto Megan's shoulder as she picked up her brother and held him in her arms. "A Fairy always knows what a child needs," Dwindle said as she looked down into Nicholas's smiling face. Megan's father smiled broadly as he remembered the Fairy from his childhood.

Megan and her father heard a noise from the backyard, and they walked over to the window to peer out. To their surprise, they saw Blaise standing before a huge snow sculpture; he was just adding the finishing touches.

"What is your cousin doing?" Megan's father asked.

Megan's eyes widened as she recognized the huge form of a Warfle. She laughed as she imagined Kharn walking around the streets of Shansymoon. Dwindle pushed open the window and zipped out into the frosty air.

"That's a nice smell," Megan's father commented.

Megan realized something. "It's babies, Dad!" Megan's father looked down at her quizzically. "Fairies smell just like babies!" she said. Megan rocked her brother gently, who now slept peacefully in her arms.

Tom Whittlebee put his arms around her. He smiled, knowing that all would be well with both of his children.

Megan looked up at him. "Dad, don't tell me a story tonight—I've got a story for you!"